CIRCULAT**D** ☑ EM(S):

Water Damage

/3 7-20-02

in the
fast
lane.

wrong turn in the fast lane.

Matt Tullos

BROADMAN
& HOLMAN
PUBLISHERS

Nashville, Tennessee

© 1998

by Matt Tullos

All rights reserved

Printed in the United States of America

0-8054-0180-6

Published by Broadman & Holman Publishers, Nashville, Tennessee

Dewey Decimal Classification: F

Subject Heading: HIGH SCHOOLS—FICTION

Library of Congress Card Catalog Number: 97-35636

Library of Congress Cataloging-in-Publication Data

Tullos, Matt, 1963–

    Wrong turn in the fast lane / Matt Tullos.

        p.   cm. — (Summit High series ; 1)

    Summary: Having found Christ in his own life, Justin has the opportunity to help his friends as well as a new student at Summit High find meaning through the Christian faith.

    ISBN 0-8054-0180-6 (tp)

    [1. Christian life—Fiction. 2. Interpersonal relations—Fiction. 3. High schools—Fiction. 4. Schools—Fiction.]   I. Title. II. Series: Tullos, Matt, 1963-   Summit High series ; 1.

      PZ7.T82316Wr   1998

      [Fic]—dc21

                                        97-35636

                                            CIP

                                              AC

1 2 3 4 5 02 01 00 99 98

Dedication

To Darlene and Danny

In the moonlit mist of a farm road just east of town, a candy apple red sports car made time. Major time. The tires scorched the blacktop road as the engine's pitch raced higher and higher, piercing the air like an arrow. Inside the car, the sound of the latest Mariah Carey CD accompanied the burning roar of the engine. The car gained speed down the straight, dusty road. With mysterious determination, like an arrow to a target, it smashed into a huge oak tree. The torrid sound of shattered glass and crushed metal followed by a loud explosion interrupted the hush of an otherwise peaceful night. The devastating collision echoed through the meadow.

The car, now an obliterated mass of twisted steel, scattered debris along the road and into a muddy ditch. The scene was horrific. The driver's body was thrown from the vehicle. Her neck was twisted and broken. Her skull was shattered and bloodied. Multiple fractures lined her small frame. Susan Stedham was dead.

⊂—H—⊃

Across town, under the bleachers of the old Summit High stadium, Tad, Troy, and Lester were flat on their backs. Lester was out cold, floating into the ozone on a combination of grass and cheap wine. Tad and Troy were trying to carry on an intelligent conversation despite the fact their brains were separated from their tongues by about a mile.

"She did what?" Troy replied as he contorted his face in utter surprise.

"She said she was open!" Tad said.

"Open? What are you talking about?" Troy said.

"She said if you'd call, she'd be open to you."

"Are you talking about a date or straight sex?"

"You really are a barbarian," Tad said laughingly.

"Hey, don't be makin' fun of my family tree." Troy said as he pitched the empty bottle that shattered on a nearby sidewalk.

"You're avoiding the offer."

"I don't have time for the dating game. Why can't we just be honest with 'em?" Troy said.

"What would you say?" Tad asked.

"I'd say 'I want sex.'"

"That only works on MTV. She'd slap you." Tad smiled, amazed at Troy's ego.

"That's stupid. Dating is just a more civilized form of prostitution. You pay the bill and you expect somethin'," Troy said and then belched.

"You won't get anywhere with Lisa by saying, 'Here's fifty bucks in cash, go buy your own lunch. Let's just get down to business—right here and now.'"

"Maybe I'm just hangin' with the wrong crowd. At least I'm not a 'Jesus freak' like Justin."

Justin Henderson, a senior at Summit High, had left the fast lane of parties and binge drinking for a different lifestyle. This created a sudden and total conflict between him and Troy's Sunday-night-under-the-bleachers drinking club. A few of Justin's other friends dragged him to a youth rally back in October. Kidnapped might be a better term. He had an experience that changed his life. He was still a leader at Summit. But anyone on campus could tell the entire direction of his life and leadership had changed. Justin, a linebacker on the football team, a utility guard on the basketball team, and president of the Key Club, also became an active member of Grove Community Church in Indianapolis.

It irked Troy. He just couldn't believe that someone could just make a choice and change their lifestyle. Sure, Troy went to church too. But it wasn't the same for him. He was soused on Saturday night and pseudo-spiritual on Sunday morning. Still, there was no hiding. Everyone knew who Troy was.

"I'm outta here," Tad said as he stumbled to his feet.

"Wait a minute, bud. We all came together." Troy said.

"I forgot."

"Who's our designated driver?" Troy asked and then cursed.

"I think it was Lester."

The boys looked over at Lester.

Tad chuckled, "He only snores when he's stoned.

Somehow I don't think he meets designated driver specs." Troy pilfered through Lester's pockets until he found Lester's keys to the truck.

Troy grabbed Lester by his shoulders. "Get his legs," he grunted to Tad. They roughly threw their friend into the bed of the pick-up. Troy and Tad jumped in laughing and mispronouncing obscenities. They would fail any breathalyzer, but they felt invincible. They had done this automotive version of Russian roulette three times this spring. So far, they had survived.

The sky was clear as a jet began its final approach to the Indianapolis International Airport. Kandi Roper was joining her mother in Indianapolis to begin a new life there. She didn't want to move from Amarillo, Texas, where she had lived all her life. Kandi's parents had ended a long family war with a bitter divorce. Her mom needed the increase in salary and the distance from Kandi's dad that a transfer to Indianapolis offered so she jumped on the opportunity. Kandi's heart pounded as she looked down at the lights of Indianapolis. Amarillo seemed light-years away as she wrote in her journal:

> *For the past few months—for most of my life, really—I've felt like a loner. I want to be happy. I want Mom to get a new start, but I didn't know it would mean a move in the middle of my junior year. I've worried so much about their marriage, Dad's drinking, and what would happen if it all fell apart. Now that it's over, I don't even know who I am anymore. I*

miss Blake. I wish he were here . . . right here on this plane. But I know he will probably never be near me again. It's time to move on. If I can just make it through the first month, maybe I'll survive.

She closed her journal and tapped her pencil nervously against the cover, frightened and yet hopeful that maybe this move would give her a chance to find an identity.

Kandi had lived for five years in an emotional battlefield, complete with threats, verbal abuse, and rage. The voices of loneliness and isolation echoed in her mind as the plane approached the runway. She didn't hide her tears since the "red eye" from DFW to Indy was almost empty. Despite this, she brushed her hair and prepared to see her mother for the first time in a month.

Back on the ground in his middle class Indianapolis home Justin tried to keep his mind on the last act of *Romeo and Juliet*. Three large stacks of books and a collection of study cards surrounded his desk which was lit by a small lamp. This late night battle against time would have to end soon. The cram session made his bed more and more inviting. He shuffled through his notes trying to make since out of the whole poison business. *Pretty far-fetched stuff, if you ask me,* he thought. *The girl's in a trance, no pulse, still alive, he thinks she's dead, so he kills himself. Not exactly a feel-good show.* His thoughts were interrupted by the phone.

"Hello?"

"Hey Justin?"

Justin said nothing still trying to figure out who the girl on the other end of the line was.

The girl laughed, "Oh come on, Justin, can't you recognize my voice? Melissa! You can be such a doofus sometimes."

Justin rolled his eyes. Melissa, the Summit High combined equivalent to the *National Enquirer* and "Melrose Place," loved being right in the middle of problems and possibilities.

"Oh, hey Melissa. How's it goin'?"

"The question is, Justin, 'how are you?'"

Justin cleared his throat trying to keep from laughing. He knew this game well. "Great. Just great."

"I heard that you and Dana broke up."

"We were never going together."

"You were dating. Right?" Melissa inquired. *Inquiring minds want to know,* she thought to herself.

"No," Justin said, "We were going out. We weren't, like, committed."

"But you aren't dating anymore."

"No, Melissa. We're not dating anymore."

"You know what I think it is?" Melissa proposed.

"No. But I have a feeling that I will really soon," Justin said.

"It's the change. Too much change all at once. I mean, I'm a Christian too, but you've got to slide into it slowly, or you're gonna make people uncomfortable. I heard she wasn't too keen on you hanging around Clipper either. Nice guy but shesh! The hair. He's really a dweeb."

"Uh . . . Thanks for the warning, Melissa, but I've been knowing the dweeb for ten years now and I kinda like him. He's a pretty nice dweeb, as dweebs go," Justin said, accenting the word *dweeb* everytime he said it.

"Touchy, touchy," Melissa crooned. "Just my opinion. Free country, you know. Anyway, I was just concerned. I'd hate for you to get frustrated with being a new Christian just because nobody dates you."

Justin pulled the phone from his ear and looked at it.

Melissa continued, "There's this girl. Her name is Marla, and she doesn't have a date to the prom and—"

Justin interrupted, "Melissa. I know Marla. She's nice. I'm flattered that you'd pay so much attention to my social status, but I'm a little more concerned about getting past *Romeo and Juliet* right now."

Clifford Hayes shot baskets outside his family's farmhouse. No one at school knew him by the name Clifford. At age three he demolished his mom's tulips with the hedge clippers. Ever since then, his family and friends referred to him as "Clipper." He tagged himself with the nickname in preschool, perhaps because Clipper was easier to pronounce. Now, a wiry six feet two inches, with red hair and freckles, Clipper pounded the concrete slab every night with a worn-out basketball.

Clipper dreamed of playing varsity for Summit but was a definite underdog. Now a starter had injured himself trying to retrieve his jock strap from the flagpole the week before. And Coach Tupper was planning an informal tryout with three or four of the junior varsity players, including Clipper.

Clipper hated free throws, a definite weakness in his game. He had been practicing them for hours before suddenly entering a fantasy time warp. His imagination transported him to the year 2004. Clipper, the underdog utility power forward who scraped his way to the top of the NBA out of sheer tenacity, now played for the Indiana Pacers. He could hear the crowd rise to their feet as they howled and whooped. He imagined the noise was so loud he could feel the vibration all the way into his bones. He saw in his mind's eye Michael Jordan, who had recently retired for the third time. Jordan was doing the play-by-play with Bob Costas. He could hear them tell the story.

Bob, straining his voice to rise above the roar of the fans, painted the picture. "I don't think I've ever seen anything like it. Have you, Michael?"

"No, Bob," Michael responded.

"Clipper Hayes has done it again! With three seconds left in the game, he steals the ball from Shaq and races down the court to lay in the basket in the final second of the game. It evens the score."

"Shaq's age is finally catching up with him," Michael said as he shook his head in sympathy.

Bob interjected, "And on top of that, Clipper was fouled and will go to the line to complete the three-point play to ice the ball game and the NBA championship."

Clipper went to the foul line (which was actually a purple chalk mark that he was constantly measuring and remarking year round). But at the moment this was not the Hayes farmhouse. This was the Market Square Arena in downtown Indianapolis.

"The pressure must be enormous," Costas continued.

Clipper had almost fooled himself into nervousness. His

heart beat a bit faster as he looked up at the basket lit by a floodlight near the garage.

Bob Costas rattled on, "Only one second left in the game. The whole season is on the line, and it comes down to this one shot. He takes a deep breath and—"

"Clipper!" A sleepy male voice yelled out to him.

"Yeah, Dad? I thought you were asleep."

"I was but I kept dreaming that I was being attacked by a bouncing ball."

Clipper laughed halfheartedly.

"Son, it's midnight! Come on in. Get some rest!"

"One more free throw and I'm done," Clipper called back to his dad. His mind returned to the play-by-play of Bob Costas and Michael Jordan.

"He's as cool as a cucumber, Bob. I don't think he has a pulse!"

Bob interrupted, "He steps up to the line!"

Clipper whispered under his breath, "Come on, baby. Come on."

Bob's voice quaked, "HE SCORES! Market Square Arena goes stark-raving mad!"

Clipper pranced around the driveway behind his home, high fiving the air. He grabbed his jacket as he started inside. In the distance he heard the faint sound of sirens.

The next morning at Summit High and the chronically over-crowded school was filled with emotion. A sound bite on a local station had summarized Susan Stedham's life in fifteen seconds. The next morning as the word spread through the faculty and student body, a cloud of stunned disbelief settled over the school. This sixteen-year-old young woman with a bright future would never walk on campus again. Why did this happen? Susan revealed her true self to few people. She had few close friends. So no one had any real answers. Though several students gathered around the flagpole at school that morning to mourn her death, life went on.

Melissa didn't know Susan Stedham that well, but she knew Kamden, Susan's closest friend. Melissa saw Kamden in the hall before first period.

"Kamden, you're here. I didn't expect to see you here. Are you OK?"

"I don't know. I'm just really numb. Just thought I needed to be here. For Susan, I mean," Kamden said.

"What happened?" Melissa asked.

Kamden glared back at her in anger. "What happened? She's dead." Kamden's eyes moistened.

"I just mean . . ." Melissa tried to be more polite. "Was there another car involved?"

"I don't know," Kamden replied.

"Did you talk to her before the accident?"

"I did. She sounded fine. Normal. Just Susan," Kamden said, looking away. "I've got to go. I don't think I can stick around here today. I didn't get much sleep last night."

When Clipper walked inside the school, he did his usual routine. The locker combination had a certain unofficial security code: 24-15-32, then a swift kick to the bottom left hand corner. It had taken him two weeks in September to perfect it. As he opened his locker, the usual cascade of personal and scholastic treasures came into view. In the spirit of *The Sound of Music,* these were a few of his favorite things. He had neither the time nor the interest to organize the four notebooks, six text books, candy wrappers, CD cases, the portable CD player, his NIV Study Bible, baseball caps, test papers, toothpicks, fifteen pens (all borrowed from Justin), twelve Jason Kidd rookie cards, super glue, three student organizers, scissors, two pairs of tennis shoes, and three pairs of athletic socks that added a unique ambiance to locker 154. Like an experienced mechanic, he began to reassemble the heap of relics in the two-cubic-foot museum.

Kandi's heart raced as she walked through the halls of Summit. It had already been a long day. She had been up since 4:30 A.M., which had given her enough time to try on almost every item in her closet. *It's bad enough to have to move for the first time in your life during your junior year,* she thought, *but in the middle of the spring semester!* She clutched her transcript and new schedule. On top of everything else, the student body was focused on the death of this girl Susan. Most just looked beyond her arrival, focusing on the tragedy.

Down the hall, Lester and Troy were weaving their way through the student body. "The car was in two pieces!" Lester exclaimed. "Our neighbor's a metro officer, and he said from the looks of it, the car was going over 100 miles an hour!"

"She must have been smashed," Troy said blandly.

"Are you kidding? Susan Stedham? No way," Lester said.

"Did she lose control?"

"Who do you think I am? The police commish?"

"Hope not," Troy said.

Tad came from behind, "Hey, did you here what happened to Susan Stedham?"

"No, we both woke up with rocks in our ears. Of course we did," Troy said smiling.

"You seem really choked up about it," Tad said sarcastically.

"We weren't close. Barely knew her. I try to stay away from girls on the debate team."

"You were sure having some Kodak moments at the Christmas party," Tad said to Troy, smiling.

"Who me?" Troy asked.

"Yes, you," Tad answered.

Troy pointed to himself, "Drunk."

"Likewise," Lester smirked.

"You guys weren't that bad off. You introduced me to her, Lester! And I can't believe you, Troy. You were hanging all over her. She even went with you for a drive."

"No recollection, your honor."

Lester shook his head and said under his breath, "What a waste."

Troy distanced himself from the topic. He was disinterested in any thought that alluded to the fragile nature of life. *That would never happen to me,* he thought.

Kandi nervously smiled as she passed the trio. As she came into Tad's sight, his eyes widened. The other two boys turned and were equally smitten. Tad timidly waved, like an overwhelmed two-year-old who spotted Goofy at Disneyland. "Check it out!"

"Must be a new student."

"You're really quick, Tad."

"Bet she's a narc."

"A narc?" Tad and Troy chimed.

"You know. A cop," Lester whispered.

"Yeah, I know what a narc is. I am just floored by your made-for-TV imagination," Troy chuckled.

At the end of third period, Kandi stopped by her locker. While she attempted to open it for the sixth time, she heard a voice just behind her.

"Hey! Trouble with the locker?"

"It feels like it's jammed," Kandi replied in frustration.

"I think these lockers were born to jam. They should've replaced them after the Civil War, but, you know, with recon- struction and all. . . ."

She smiled nervously and looked away.

"The trick is finding the sweet spot," he said as he probed the locker like a bomb specialist.

"The sweet spot?" Kandi asked.

"Like people, every locker is vulnerable. The secret is find- ing its weakness. Try entering your combination again," he said, then asked, "You're new here, aren't you?"

She nodded her head as she twirled the dial.

"I'm Justin," he said as he stuck out his hand in a business- like manner. She just kept twirling. Justin dropped his hand.

"Now don't lift the handle yet," Justin said as he focused himself. "The bottom looks off balance."

"It does?"

"Yep," Justin pointed to his face. "Trained eyes."

Wham! He punched the locker and it burst open. Kandi jumped back, then laughed.

"I have a brown belt," Justin said in a serious tone.

"Really?"

"Sure," he said as he pointed to his leather belt.

She laughed again, politely.

A long silence filled the air as they awkwardly looked at each other and smiled.

"I'm Justin."

"I know. You said that."

"Oh . . . right."

More silence.

"Do you have a name?" Justin asked inquisitively.

"Uh yeah. As a matter of fact, I do. I'm Kandi."

"Nice to meet you. Where're you from?"

"Amarillo, Texas."

"Is that anywhere near Houston?" Justin asked.

"Uh . . . nope."

"I was just wondering because our youth group went to Houston, but Texas is a big state. The biggest."

"Next to Alaska," Kandi added.

"Right. Next to Alaska. I was about to say that."

Justin thought, *I've never bombed on first impressions as bad as this. This day will live in infamy. 'Texas is a big state, huh.' Major duh.* "Have you found a church yet?" Justin said while thinking, *May Day! May Day! Geek factor is rising by the second!*

"Church? No. I—," She stopped to calculate her response. "I'm Catholic and I think that you just go to the temple . . . I mean the church that's closest to you."

At that moment, Clipper walked up and slapped Justin on the back. "Justin! Whusup? This is the big day!"

"What?"

"The tryout?" Clipper said.

"Oh yeah. See you then," Justin replied, trying to shoo him away for the moment.

"I practiced my free throw and my jump shot all weekend. I even hit twelve in a row. Can you believe it?" Clipper said.

"That's great. I'll see you at practice."

"Tupper wants the three J.V. players who are up for the spot there about thirty minutes early," Clipper continued.

"Great. Then I'll see you when I—"

Clipper looked over at Kandi. "Hi! I'm Clipper. What's your name?"

"Kandi."

"Nice to meet you, Kandi. You're new here aren't you?"

Kandi thought, *If somebody says that again, I'm going to scream.*

"Hey Justin, I need to ask you something. Can we talk for a second?" Clipper inquired.

"We are talking," Justin said.

"I mean—," he cut a glance toward Kandi.

Kandi looked around and said, "I'd better find the music building."

"It's outside," Clipper replied.

"I thought it might be," Kandi exhaled and rolled her eyes.

"See you, Kandi," Justin said with a smile.

Kandi, genuinely amused by the whole encounter, replied, "Nice to meet you."

As she blended into the mass of students scurrying to beat the bell, Justin called out, "Remember. Hit the locker on the bottom left-hand corner."

"Gotcha," Kandi called back with one thumb up.

"Let me know if you need anything," Justin offered as she disappeared.

"Thanks."

"Hey!" Clipper said coolly, "I can feel vibes. This is good."

Justin growled at Clipper, "What is it, Clipper? What's so desperately important that you—"

"Reebok or Nike?"

"What!?"

"Reebok or Nike?" Clipper repeated.

"Wear what you brought," Justin said.

"I brought both."

"Good grief, Clipper! Is that the all-important question you had to ask me? That was really rude! This is her first day at school, and you practically kicked her out of the conversation," Justin said with a twinge of exasperation in his voice.

"I just want to fit in to the scheme of the team and first impressions are—"

"I came within an inch of inviting her to my house for the Bible study next week."

"Ouch," Clipper said as his face tensed, "I guess I blew it."

"No big deal," Justin surrendered, half smiling. "Her locker's a tough one. She'll be back."

Melissa loved to meet people and committed her energies into installing all new students into their appropriate cliques. To Melissa, Kandi became a perfect client for her free service. *No problem fitting her in,* Melissa thought.

"So did you have a guy in Amarillo?" Melissa asked.

Kandi smiled, humored by Melissa's Barbara Walters demeanor, "Yes, I had a guy in Amarillo."

"Pen pals now, I guess," Melissa said.

"I don't know. Not exactly sure what'll happen there. We said we'd keep in touch but . . ."

"I know," Melissa interrupted. "This ain't Hollywood. I had a boyfriend who moved to Gary, Indiana. We wrote three times. Called each other once or twice. E-mailed a few other times. It fizzles pretty fast."

Kandi wanted to change the subject, "What happened with this girl who died the other night?"

"I don't know. Susan was smart. I heard somebody say she offed herself," Melissa said.

"Why?"

"Nobody knows the reason. I think she may have just freaked out and lost control of the car. She hung out with the debate eggheads, went to a few parties, but she wasn't the kind to get loaded and slam into a tree. Not very many people really knew her or at least nobody really got into her brain. I talked with a real close friend of hers this morning. Totally clueless. It's Sherlock stuff. Way over my head."

After school Clipper joined the other two prospects for varsity basketball practice. No one could deny that Clipper could rebound. Lanky? Yes. Clumsy? Yes. But he had a nose for the ball. He knew where it would land if someone missed a shot. Probably because he had missed so many shots in his own backyard. And those elbows! They were as sharp as cue sticks, and when he got his grip on the ball and started swinging those lethal bone protrusions, everyone on the court would run away, even his teammates. This impressed the coaches. They definitely needed a rebounder. The elbows were an added benefit. But of course you have to do more than rebound to be on a high school basketball team. That was the problem.

"If only he could pass, dribble, and shoot," Coach Tupper whispered to his assistant, Lunsford.

"He's awful feisty," Lunsford added.

"We don't have time for grooming a player like Clipper. Post-season play starts in three weeks," Tupper said.

"Lester looks good, but we already have four guards."

Their conversation was interrupted as a player screamed out, "Hey, watch it with the elbows! You almost took my head off!"

Lunsford shouted out to the other side of the court, "Way to hustle, Clipper."

Tupper chuckling shook his head, "He'd make a great mascot."

Tupper blew his whistle and called the team together. Then the three possible replacements shot free throws. Tim, a fairly talented freshman, made six of ten free throws. Lester—nine of ten. Then came Clipper.

Just be cool, Clipper thought. *You're in the backyard. Just you and the ball. It's midnight. It's you, the ball, and your incredible wrist action that gives the ball its unique rotation. No big deal. Piece-o-cake. Nothing but net.* But then a rush of panic and intimidation shot through his veins, and his thought pattern took a 180-degree turn. *WHO AM I KIDDING!!!! It's the moment I've been waiting for. Another chance at varsity. I've got to hit these free throws!*

He could only pray for more smooth swishes through the hoop's clean white webbing than awkward doinks on to the rim. Clipper had the kind of shooting mechanism that if he drew any iron off the rim the ball would rarely bounce into the basket. So he whispered a prayer, *Lord, don't let it hit the rim.* His prayers were answered. The good news was he didn't hit the rim. The bad news was that he hit nothing. The first shot fell a good two inches short of the basket. Clipper's freckled face turned beet red. His prayers went from, *Nothing but net.* to *Anything! Let me hit anything!*

Tad and Troy feasted on the moment.

"Can anybody say choke?" Tad said.

"The purpose of this exercise, Clipper, is to throw the ball into the hoop," Troy said in a pseudo-intellectual tone.

The gym echoed with laughter and snorts.

"Clam it up guys or you'll be doing laps all over town," Tupper shouted.

Clipper's perception of himself was at an all-time low and it showed. Although Clipper was an energetic guy, full of jokes and one liners, he was blown down by any light wind of shame or criticism.

As Clipper's second free throw hit the rim twice and bounded away from the goal, Justin turned to Tad and Troy, "Why can't you guys grow up?"

"Excuse me, Right Reverend Billy Graham," Troy retorted.

"Typical class . . ." Justin said under his breath.

Clipper. Third attempt. Brick.

Clipper's mind raced in a million different directions. Three attempts. None successful. In a matter of seconds, he went from a feeling of optimism to utter embarrassment. He whispered to himself, "All things . . . All things, . . ." the secret slogan he and Justin adopted. Fighting for his reputation, he let the fourth shot go. It bounded off the backboard and into the basket. It was a fluke triumph that drained the panicked blush from Clipper's face. He felt a twinge of confidence as he hurled the fifth. It, too, dropped in.

"Way to hang in there, Clipper!" Justin yelled out.

"Wow. Two in a row. Let's call the president," Troy mocked, unemotionally.

Clipper made four of ten and felt somewhat redeemed after missing the first three; yet he felt like his chances of making varsity vanished that afternoon. He was nervous throughout the practice and it showed. The only positive thing that he could point to out of the experience was that he was in good condition and he hustled. Did he ever. He dove for loose balls and blocked a couple of shots out of sheer will. He got any rebound he had a chance to get. And of course the elbows were an added bonus. But basketball required offense too. On offense he thought he looked more like a middle-school student than a junior in high school. He had a prayer and that was just about it. What was in front of him after the tryout was forty-eight hours of not knowing. For Clipper, that was almost as much torture as not making the team.

The sight of Kandi waiting outside the guys' locker room that evening completely took Justin by surprise. He had thought about her off and on all day. He recounted their first awkward encounter with a strange combination of delight and embarrassment. It wasn't easy to plan how to "just run into someone," nevertheless that's what he had been doing all day. During Algebra II, Chemistry, and even basketball practice he plotted every path that might lead to her locker. He rehearsed in his mind casual, humorous remarks he could make when they met. These would be passing comments that would sound intelligent and yet inviting. Through the day, he would catch himself and think, *What am I doing? I don't even know the girl, and I'm already wondering what it'd be like to hold her hand*

and walk through the park with her. He'd shake his head, smile, then grit his teeth, and focus in on the present. Then thirty seconds later he'd be back to that imaginary park with Kandi, a girl he barely knew.

But there before him stood Kandi. He was dumbfounded and a little self-conscious. This was definitely not in the script! Neither was his wet hair, sloppy sweats, and ragged duffel bag. But he tried to make the best of it.

"Hi Kandi. It is Kandi, isn't it?" (He knew good and well what her name was. He just wanted to hide the fact that she had been trapped inside his brain all day.)

"Oh hi! You're uh—"

"Justin."

"Right, 'Justin.' The locker opener."

"How was your first day? Are you gettin' used to everything?"

"It was pretty good as first days go, you know."

"Were you able to get into your uh—"

"Locker? Yes. I kicked the bottom just like you showed me and presto—it opened."

"I'm impressed. Not too shabby for a first timer."

Things were going better than he had dreamed. He couldn't believe she appeared right in front of him. *Why is she here?* he thought as they talked. *Could she have come here just to finish the conversation that Clipper barged in on this morning? Nah . . . But maybe. Maybe so!*

As she talked about Amarillo, where she came from, Justin smiled, listening intently. Kandi had charmed him completely. And then during a lull in the conversation, he seized the moment.

"Hey Kandi, if you're not busy next Monday night, we have this Bible study at my house and I thought you might—"

Just then, Troy walked out of the guys' locker room.

"Kandi. Thanks for waiting for me," Troy said. "Sorry it took me so long. Didn't want to go home lookin' like old Justin here. Great practice, huh pal? I think Lester's a shoe-in for the final spot on the varsity. Don't you?"

The sudden realization stunned Justin. He went from Mount Everest to Death Valley in a split second. Kandi was not milling around the locker room to see him. She came to meet *Troy,* of all people. His heart sank.

"So where do you want to eat, Kandi?"

Kandi stared blankly at Justin. She didn't even hear the question. She too felt awkward about the situation. Then realizing what Troy said, she responded, "Whatever. I don't know. I just got here."

"We have these great things in Indy. They're incredible. They're called steaks." Troy laughed heartily at his own joke as Kandi smiled and rolled her eyes.

"I'd invite you too, Justin, but I think we can make it through supper without a chaplain," Troy said.

Justin, being a good sport, chuckled and started walking away as he said, "Sure. You two have fun."

"That we will, my friend," Troy called out as he and Kandi walked toward his '98 Camero. "That we will."

Just after nine o'clock, Kandi and Troy pulled into Kandi's apartment parking lot from their date. They had eaten at the Longhorn Eatery at Market Square in downtown Indianapolis. At first, she kept asking herself why she agreed to go out with a guy she barely knew. She also felt awkward about the conversation outside the locker room with Justin. She liked Justin. But by the end of the evening with Troy, she felt her inhibitions with him dissolve. They had a great night, and she was glad she had gone.

They walked from the parking lot to Kandi's apartment. Well-groomed shrubs and flower beds adorned the Springwater Apartments. Stars decorated the brisk night sky.

"So where are we going?" Troy asked.

Kandi laughed shyly, "We're just walking."

"You *do* live here, don't you?" Troy said as he took her hand.

"Of course I live here." She looked at her hand webbed in his. "So what are *you* doing?"

"I'm holding your hand. It's a tradition in Indiana."

"Really," she said.

"We have a lot of great traditions here," Troy replied casually, mysteriously.

"I think I'd better wait on the other traditions."

They both laughed.

Kandi led Troy along the cement trails lit by small lamps. They meandered through small gardens and past the sparkling pool. Somewhere in the simple acts of walking and talking, Kandi began to sense a magical intimacy to the night. She felt a sense of belonging that she hadn't felt in years. It was like a dream. *And to think I had to fly almost a thousand miles to feel this way,* she thought. A new world opened before her. As her eyes glanced down at the face of her watch, she felt the cold splash of reality. It was 11:00!

She interrupted Troy mid-sentence, "I think I'd better go. Mom's going to kill me. Look, I'll see you tomorrow." She took a few steps away from him.

"Whoa, Whoa," he interjected, "You're not getting off that easy. Let me walk you to your apartment," Troy said.

"Troy! It's eleven. Isn't it past your bedtime, sweety?"

Troy rolled his eyes, "It's early! Walk with me."

"Thanks," she paused, "but no thanks. Hey listen. I had a great time."

"Suit yourself. Can I call you?" he asked.

"I'll see you tomorrow."

Kandi was walking a few inches off the ground as she approached the door, but she didn't have to open it. Sylvia Roper was there waiting for her.

"Where have you been? I haven't heard from you since 5:00!"

"I told you, I met some friends."

"You said you were going to be home before eight. But this is ridiculous. I was an inch away from calling the police, the morgue—"

"Come on, Mom. Give me a break."

"No, you give *me* a break!" Sylvia shouted back.

"You should be glad that I met some friends. You didn't set a time for me to be back. I thought you said you trusted me."

"I thought I did."

The glimmer of a romantic evening quickly faded into battle between mother and daughter. Kandi exploded. She knew she had came in late, but she really expected her mom to be excited that she had a life outside Amarillo, Texas. Sure she told half truths. She didn't go out with friends. She went out with one friend. But still, nothing happened. They didn't even kiss. She couldn't have asked for a more memorable night. She finally had hope things were going to be better in Indiana. *Why is Mom doing this to me?* she wondered.

Kandi tightened her jaw. "Why can't you just let me be happy for once? Why can't you trust me?! I thought this is what you wanted. You said I'd make new friends here and things would be better. You move me halfway across the country in the middle of the semester, away from Dad, who I'll probably only get to see once a year if I'm lucky, and you expect me to—"

Kandi's mom grabbed her by the shoulders and looked squarely in her eyes, "Do you have any memory whatsoever about what life was like before your Dad and I split up? That's not fair! You know the hell we've been through with him. How can you even say that?!"

Tears filled Kandi's eyes as she jerked herself away from her mother's clutches. "Leave me alone." She ran to her room. "Just stay away from me!" The door slammed.

Kandi fell to her bed surrounded by boxes and packing paper and buried her face in a pillow. She felt the darkness and gloom that had been her traveling companions for the past two years. Heaving sobs filled the dark room. They came from the very depths of her heart. Kandi knew her mom was right. They had needed to move. In her mind's eye she revisited a memory so traumatic and graphic she could never forget it.

It happened on a cold October evening in Amarillo. Kandi's dad stumbled into the house at 10:30. Like many nights, he had spent his evening downing half a bottle of scotch.

It was crystal clear when her father's slide began. He had lost his job during a major corporate down-sizing. He watched two people he had hired move up the ladder. Later the two forced him out completely. It cut him to the core. He searched for a painkiller and found one in alcohol. But the painkiller became a man-killer, which threatened not only his life but those around him. In the epicenter of this upheaval were Kandi and Sylvia.

"If you're that mad at me, why don't you just pack it up and leave. But take that little flirt of a daughter with you!" he yelled.

"Please keep your voice down," Kandi's mom pleaded. "Why are you doing this to us?"

"You've been seeing someone else behind my back haven't you?" he said.

"What?"

"Don't give me that. You know what I'm talking about, Sylvia! Admit it!"

"How dare you even think that!"

Kandi, awakened by the sound of fighting, came into the kitchen, her eyes filled with tears. Mr. Roper grabbed her chin and in a half whisper hissed, "What's his name, Kandi? Your mom's lover. You know him, don't you?"

"Stop it!" Sylvia cried hysterically. "Stop it this instant."

Without hesitation Gary backhanded his wife hard across the face. The blow drew blood, and Kandi ran to her mother, who fell to the floor. She tried to shield Sylvia while through tears she cringed and called out to her dad, "Leave us alone. Go away, Daddy. I hate you!"

Gary immediately jerked Kandi up from the floor. She felt as if he could tear her arm off if he wanted to do it. She shrieked in pain as her mom mumbled and moaned in a trance of trauma. His fingers were locked around Kandi's tender biceps as he walked over to his briefcase that contained a precarious combination of resumes, letters of recommendations, a half-devoured bottle of scotch whiskey, and a handgun. He grabbed the gun and threw Kandi into the wall. He pressed her against the wall with his forearm and put the gun up to her head.

"Leave her alone, Gary!" Sylvia yelled as she ran to Kandi's aid. "What is happening to you?" Gary swung the gun across Sylvia's collarbone. She fell to the floor, writhing in pain.

"You stay out of this!" Then he turned the gun back on Kandi.

He pressed the cold barrel against her hot forehead, as she moaned, "Please, Daddy, no, please, Daddy. I'm sorry. Don't shoot me, Daddy. Please . . . Don't shoot."

Gary cocked the trigger. "You don't have to tell me that you hate me. I know it. I know it, little girl."

"No, Daddy. I'm sorry."

"Three bullets. That's all I need. Three bullets would solve all our problems," he said, still pressing Kandi against the wall. Then he pulled the gun from her temple and wrapped his lips around the end of the barrel and distorted his face as if preparing for the very end.

Kandi trembled and plead, "We love you, Daddy! Please don't do this."

"Oh God, no," Sylvia prayed to the God she never knew.

"We love you, Daddy. Please . . . Please . . ."

In a state of mental comatose, he looked at his daughter. And slowly squeezed the trigger.

Click.

But for the absence of a bullet in that certain chamber of the gun, the family would have made the morning news the following day. Instead, they were left with a deep and private memory that would follow them like a secret ghost.

And now in Indianapolis, hundreds of miles and thousands of hours from those dark days, Kandi embraced those horrible memories like a strange friend.

As Justin walked toward the entrance of the Summit gym morning, he saw Clipper asleep next to the door. "Hey, scrawny dude! Wake up!" Justin said as he lightly kicked Clipper on the hip, "What are you doing here? Mom kicked you out of the house?"

"Oh," Clipper replied, opening his eyes and stretching his back from the nap. "I must have fallen asleep."

"I'd say so. What's the deal?"

"You do know what day it is, don't you?"

"Thursday."

Clipper rolled his eyes, "I know it's Thursday, think again."

"Oh, I forgot. It's decision day for the final spot. How long have you been here?" Justin asked.

"I got up at four."

"Four in the morning! What for? I know that Tupper's a Christian, but he's not that spiritual," Justin said.

"I couldn't sleep at home, plus I wanted to be the first to see the notice. I didn't want to walk over to the bulletin board with everyone gawking at me while I checked out the roster. That's embarrassing. Everyone looking at you, judging how you're going to look after you've just missed the team for the fourth time . . . I'd rather look at the roster and weep privately."

"Why look at the board if you've already cut yourself out of contention?" Justin said.

"I didn't do that this morning. I did it Monday night at the practice, remember? Four out of ten at the line! I choked, Justin."

"But they aren't looking for just a free-throw shooter. You were a hoss out there."

"I *felt* like a hoss. A hoss in a china cabinet."

"You rebounded. You blocked Meeker's jump shot."

"They weren't even looking. They had their backs turned when I did that."

There was a lull in the conversation as Justin searched for something positive to say. "You almost took my eye out with your right elbow. That should be worth something, shouldn't it? I mean, I don't want to risk life and limb for a rebound with those lethal weapons flailing around."

Coach Lunsford interrupted the two as he jingled his keys, "'Scuse me guys." He walked between Justin and Clipper to unlock the door. "Model students this morning? You're here before me. Swell."

Clipper and Justin looked at each other, perplexed, pondering the term: *swell*.

Lunsford eyes widened as he said, "Oh right, it's the big day. You're here to see if you made the team, right Clipper?

"So, did I?"

Lunsford shrugged his shoulders, "I don't know."

"Oh come on. You know," Justin said wryly.

"No, Justin. I really don't know. We are going to go pull a name out of a hat in a second," Lunsford continued.

"You're joking."

Lunsford gave no response. He just opened the door and walked on.

"Of course I'm kidding," he finally yelled back to them. "I left the choice up to Tupper. He made the call so I really don't know." The three stared at each other for a moment and finally Lunsford said, "So what are you waiting for?"

They both took the long walk to the end of the hall.

"Slow down, Justin," Clipper said.

"Don't you want to see?" Justin asked.

"Of course I want to see," Clipper replied.

"You're strange. You know that? First you get here at four in the morning to see the list, and now you don't want me to rush down the hall when the doors open," Justin said.

As Clipper approached the bulletin board, things began to go in slow motion. It was the most critical moment in his life. He had always dreamed of playing basketball for Summit High, ever since his dad took him to the games when he was five. He could imagine bursting into the Summit High School gym surrounded by a thousand screaming fans. To him, that was half the thrill—to be a part of the team, to belong to a group that was striving for something important. He worked hard all last summer, knowing that if he didn't make the team this year, he would probably never have a chance to play on a legitimate basketball team again. In his mind, this was one of those defining moments in life. He tried not to think of it that way, but he couldn't help it.

Justin and Clipper looked at the board, scanning the lunchroom notices, cheerleading practice schedules, personal sale items.

"There it is," Justin said. Even *he* felt nervous.

"You read the notice. I can't look at it," Clipper said as he walked away from the board.

Justin took a deep breath, and read, "As you may know, there has been a vacancy on the varsity basketball team due to Ralph Edmunson's knee injury . . . yada, yada, yada . . ."

"No 'yadas' Justin. The whole banana! Read the whole thing," Clipper said as he paced back and forth.

"We offered three players on the junior varsity squad an opportunity to scrimmage with varsity to appraise how each individual's talent would fit into the chemistry of the team. This was a tough choice that was discussed by the entire varsity staff. We are pleased to announce that Clipper Hayes will be—"

"What did you say?" Clipper barely whispered.

Justin smiled, "Clipper Hayes!"

"Let me see that. We are pleased to announce that Clipper Hayes will be moved to the varsity team!!" Clipper read, screaming.

"Congratulations . . ."

"I made it! I made it! I MADE IT!! Is this a dream?"

"It's not a dream," Justin said.

"Typo?"

"Pretty mammoth typo, if it is one."

Much to his chagrin, Justin knew that there was a big, unbridled bear hug somewhere in this litany with his name on it. He was not mistaken. Clipper threw his arms around Justin, picked him up, and twirled him around. Justin breathed a sigh of relief that no one saw this sappy display of male bonding. Clipper didn't stop there. He burst into Lunsford's office. "Thank you! Thank you! I'm not going to let you down. I can promise you that!"

"Well you won't get very much playing time. You do realize that, don't you?" Lunsford said.

"I do. But if you need me in the clutch, I'll be there."

"I'm sure you will, Clipp—" Lunsford said.

"Just to your right—" Clipper continued.

"That's really comforting to—" Lunsford said, smiling.

"You just call out my name—"

"Seems like that's from a song or something . . ." Justin said to himself as he stood outside Lunsford's door.

"This is one of the greatest things that—" Clipper stopped mid-sentence. "My Dad! I've gotta go tell my dad. He's gonna freak!"

"I don't think you have time, homeroom is—" Lunsford warned.

"Fifteen minutes. I can do this. I can do this!" Clipper shouted.

Clipper burst out of Lunsford's office and passed Justin as he jetted out toward his car.

"You won't make it back before the bell!" Justin cried out as he felt the breeze from Clipper's afterburners.

"Sure I will!" Clipper shouted back.

"Why don't you just call him?" Justin asked.

"No way. This is face-to-face news!" Clipper blurted out, enthusiastically.

"Can't you wait till this afternoon? Homeroom's in fifteen minutes!" Justin called out.

Clipper didn't even slow down. "This I can do!"

"The school zone! Don't forget the school zone! They'll lock you up and throw away the key," Justin reminded him loudly.

"Lighten up, Justin. I'm a model citizen!" Clipper screamed back.

"Fifteen miles an hour!!" Justin called out, giving Clipper a half wave. As he watched Clipper exit the parking lot, he asked himself, "When did I become my dad?"

As he turned onto the street, Justin could faintly hear Clipper over the hubub of the morning traffic, "All things, Justin! All things!"

It had been two days since Kandi and her mom had the blowup over her late arrival. They avoided conversation at home, barely looking at each other, more out of shame than anger. They desperately needed to talk, support, and forgive, but there had been so much hurt over the past few years. They had seen a successful, confident man evolve into an angry predator. They loved him, yet they could do nothing to stop the pain that dominated his life. After he lost the job, he became like a caged lion, pacing back and forth, humiliated by the captivity of his bleak future. The drinking, the shouting, the mental and emotional abuse seemed to flow out of a bottomless pit.

It wasn't just the loss of employment. Things had been brewing under the surface for years. Kandi remembered being awakened in the middle of the night by angry words and threats when she was just three or four. She would always find herself caught in the middle of a fight, praying

that things would change. And they *did* change from time
to time. There were wonderful memories when they were
at peace. The house would be filled with laughter and
harmony, but even in the good times, Kandi always seemed to
know that behind the shadows lurked the monsters of rage
and loneliness.

It was Friday evening when Kandi finally cut the small talk.
"Mom, I'm sorry. I should have called you the other night."

Her mom smiled. "You didn't want to call because you
were afraid that I'd say no."

"Maybe so. I just wanted to fit in and—"

"You were with a guy, weren't you?"

Kandi wondered whether she should tell her mom the truth
or continue the charade about being with a group. She decided to take the risk of being scorned. She wanted so desperately to talk to her mom about Troy.

"If you promise you won't kill me."

Her mom smiled and nodded.

"His name is Troy," Kandi's eyes widened slightly. "He's on
the basketball team. You'd really like him."

"So this was a date," Mrs. Roper looked concerned.

"Mom, we didn't do anything. We just went out to eat. It
was wonderful. Can you believe it? The first day of school, and
I meet a guy."

"So that's the guy who's been calling every hour."

Kandi rolled her eyes.

Her mom conceded, "OK. Not every hour." She paused for
a moment, "Every *other* hour."

Kandi looked away, "Mom, I'm sorry about Monday night."

"It's OK. Just don't do that to me again, or you're dead meat," Mom said, smiling.

"I wonder how Dad is."

"I do too," Sylvia said, stroking her daughter's short black hair.

"It's so peaceful, you know? Being away from him . . . But you know what's strange?"

Sylvia shook her head.

"After all that he's put us through—the drinking, the anger, the abuse—I just feel empty . . . like I'm not all here." Tears welled up in Kandi's eyes as she looked away from her mom. "It scares me to death. I know you did what you had to do, and I sure wouldn't want to live with him, but after all was said and done—after you got the transfer, the divorce and the whole nightmare was over—I'm scared because I still love him."

Kandi and Sylvia embraced as Kandi's fragile shoulders trembled with soft uncontrollable sobs.

"Believe it or not, Kandi, I love him too. You've got his eyes, girl. And every time I look at you, I see a piece of him."

As the embrace broke, Kandi wiped her eyes. "Mom, do you ever wonder what it's all about?"

"What do you mean?"

"Our life. It just seems like it's a big joke that some god has played on us. It's one problem after another."

"You sound like such a pessimist."

"I guess I am, Mom. Pessimist, realist, or something . . . I just have a hard time believing that there's any rhyme or reason. It just seems like we're all alone on this planet. It's sink or swim," Kandi said.

"Eat or be eaten?"

"I hope not." They both laughed.

⊂–‖–⊃

In a deserted stretch of land just outside of town, Troy, Lester, and Tad were camping. "Don't drop it! I worked five hours today to buy it." Tad said as Lester rolled the joint.

"Cool your jets, man. It's a masterpiece."

Lester lit it and took a deep drag.

"That's some consolation prize for missing out on the varsity," Troy commented while laying on the ground looking at the stars.

"Who gives a rip, anyway," Lester said as he coughed and exhaled.

"I do," said Troy angrily. "We got Bullwinkle. I'm telling you, if he gets on the court, he'll embarrass us all. He'll trip over the baseline paint or hit his head on the bench. He's a walkin' accident. The only thing he can do is rebound."

"See if I care," Lester said as he stared into the fire. "How's the new conquest goin', Troy?"

"Kandi? She'll take a little more time than most," Troy said sarcastically.

"I was really honored that you dropped the new project for a night, so that you could join us," Lester said.

"It's important to be on your best behavior for a little while. Until they're ga-ga. And then you go in for the kill. You've got to get their trust before you can get what you want."

Tad laughed, "As Mom says, 'You've got to eat the spinach before you get dessert.'"

"Your mom's a smart chick."

Lester looked over at Troy, "So what's the spinach?"

"Flowers, long walks, lies about how interesting they are, cards, whatever it is that they want. You've got to soften them up. In the meantime, I've got to sow my wild oats somehow. That's where you come in. Kandi probably thinks we're eating s'mores and singing 'Kum-by-ya.' Hey! Give me a hit on that thing. Where's the beer anyway? Weed dries me out."

This was Troy's strategy. He continued his charade as the all-state model citizen. He saw Kandi as a perfect target. She walked right into his web, totally unaware of Troy's double life. To her, he was a person who deeply cared for her. She shared a little more with him each time they talked. He listened intently, which was something her father never seemed to be able to do between work and the personal demons he constantly fought.

When they went out Saturday night, Kandi introduced Troy to her mom, who was equally charmed by his smile.

"So what are you going to do about it?" Clipper asked Justin. They had just left the church Sunday afternoon and were headed to Clipper's house for dinner. Justin drove while Clipper gave him the third degree.

"You ask me that question like I'm the date cop! I can't go blow the whistle on everybody who has a bad reputation."

"You like her, don't you?"

"I don't even know the girl!" Justin exclaimed.

"That's not true. You've talked to her," Clipper replied.

"True. I think that I could legitimately say that I know her, but every time I start a decent conversation, someone else barges in."

"Are you still carrying a grudge about what happened the other day?"

"I was just kidding, Clipper. Look, I barely know her. I was genuinely uh—"

"Attracted?"

"Would you stop filling in the blanks every time I take a breath. OK. I'll say it myself. I was attracted to her."

"So back to square one: What are you gonna do?" Clipper asked.

"Nothing, Clip, nothing! What do you expect me to say. 'Hey, Kandi, I'm Justin, the locker fixer. Remember me? I know we don't know each other that well, but I feel obligated to tell you that Troy's bad news. Some people even go so far as to call him a creep. A love-taker. Heart-breaker. Cake-baker. Why don't you stop this thing before it gets out of hand and date . . . say . . . ME!'"

On Monday morning, Melissa saw Kamden in the hall. Kamden had missed five days of school, and she didn't look well at all. Melissa knew the grief of Susan Stedham's death had taken its toll on her. She looked pale and emaciated.

Melissa walked up to her and hugged her, but Kamden remained stiff and unresponsive.

"It's good to see you. I've been worried."

"I went out of town for a few days and stayed with my dad. The counselor said that it might be best for me to take some time away. But I walk in here, and it all comes flooding back." Kamden stopped and wiped a tear from her cheek. "I don't think I'll ever be able to come back here without remembering Susan. I'm just not doing that good."

"How are Susan's parents?" Melissa asked.

"They're just shocked. They still don't understand what happened."

"Do you know what happened? I mean, why this happened?" Melissa asked, trying to conceal her gnawing curiosity.

Kamden looked away, swallowed, then spoke, "I've got to go."

"What happened?" Melissa said persistently.

"What difference does it make to you?" Kamden said, becoming more angry. "It's not for anyone to know. It's none of your business!"

"I'm not trying to be nosy. I just—"

Kamden interrupted her, "Just leave me alone! And let Susan rest in peace."

⊂—H—⊃

Justin had a plan as he walked on campus. If he ran into Kandi, he'd invite her to the Bible study again. He'd play it cool. He only wished that he had some way of making her feel at ease about coming. He fantasized walking up to her and saying mechanically, "This is not a date. Repeat. This is not a date. Several students will gather at my house to discuss the Bible. Repeat, this is not a date."

Right after lunch, the opportunity was there. Justin walked casually by as if he didn't see her (but of course he had). He took a deep nervous breath and prayed silently, sincerely, *OK God, don't let me say anything stupid.* "Hey Kandi. How's everything going?"

"Going great!" Kandi replied.

"I'm Justin."

"Right."

"Are you finding your way around OK?" Justin asked.

"Whew, it's kind of been tough, midsemester and all."

"Hey, I was just wondering if you'd like to come to a Bible study at my house."

"A what?"

"A Bible study," Justin said.

"You mean like me and you?" Kandi asked tentatively.

"Yes . . . I mean no . . . Actually there are a bunch of us who meet every Monday night around 7:30—"

Kandi interrupted, "Well, sounds interesting. I don't know. I don't think I told you. Of course I didn't, but maybe you noticed, Troy and I have been—"

"I know, Kandi," Justin's smile calmed her. "He's welcome to come too." Justin couldn't believe what he was saying, but something inside really gave him the desire for Troy to come. "It'd be a great way for you to meet some more of us."

"Can I call you?" She flinched slightly, "I mean, about directions if I decide to come?"

"You bet. Here's my number." Justin scribbled his number on yellow legal pad paper. "Hope you can make it!"

He walked away with a grin on his face and a prayer of thanksgiving on his lips. *I don't think I sounded too much like a dork. Thanks, God!*

Almost like clockwork, as soon as school was dismissed for the day, a storm cloud blanketed Summit High and surrounding areas with a cold March rain. As students scurried to cars and buses, Kandi saw Troy swing by in his car. His passenger side front window rolled down, and he called out to her as she walked on the covered walkway to the busses.

"Hey, Beautiful. Goin' my way?"

"And which way are you going?" she asked with a grin.

"The Springwater Apartments."

Kandi smiled coyly, "What a coincidence. That's where I live."

"Well now, that *is* a coincidence. Hop in. I'll give you a ride."

"I don't know. Mom always told me not to accept rides from strangers."

"It's always worth the risk. Sure beats taking the bus. I've got better CDs."

"You convinced me." She ran over to his Camero as he popped open the passenger door, the rain drenching her in just the few seconds between the walkway and the car. She dove in the car and then playfully shook her wet hair.

"Cut it out, Kandi! So that's the thanks I get for rescuing you."

Kandi laughed, then leaned over to him, kissing him. Troy looked at her with a deep inquisitive look. "What's the matter?" Kandi asked.

Troy just chuckled and shifted the car into drive. "Hey, I have an idea. Why don't we go get some ice cream or something. You wanna?"

"I'd better call my—"

He tossed her a cell phone from his glove compartment.

"I'm impressed." She dialed the number. "Ms. Roper, please?" During the long pause, Troy divided his attention between the road and Kandi. He reached over and lightly squeezed her shoulder.

"Hey, Mom," Kandi said nervously.

"Where are you?" Sylvia asked.

"I'm in Troy's car. We want to know if it's all right for me to go with him to get some ice cream."

"Ask her if you can come over for supper after that. You haven't even met my parents yet," Troy suggested.

"Troy wants to know if I can eat supper with him at his place. He wants me to meet his mom and dad."

"So you're sure that they'll be there with you two."

Kandi rolled her eyes, "Mom, what did I just say. That's the whole point! To meet his parents . . ."

"OK. I guess that's OK. You sure you don't want me to come too?"

"Mom."

"Just joking," Sylvia said.

"So?"

"I guess that's fine. This is a major trust test for you."

"I'll be good."

"And Troy?" Sylvia asked.

Kandi paused and then said, "If he starts getting facial hair and fangs while we're out, I'll come straight home."

Troy laughed.

Sylvia replied, "Very funny. . . . "I don't know, hon. Ice cream and then supper? This younger generation. What will they think of next? I'm expecting you back by seven."

"7:00?!"

"7:00. Period."

"8:00?" Kandi pleaded.

"7:00."

"7:30?"

"7:15. Case closed."

"Wow a whole fifteen minutes more," Kandi said.

"Don't mess with me, little girl," Sylvia said.

"Love you, Mom."

"Yeah, right. See you at 7:15."

Kandi put the phone back into the glove compartment. She turned to Troy. "So where's the ice cream in this town?" She asked.

"Oh, you know, we really shouldn't spoil our appetite," he said slyly, with sarcasm.

"So what now . . . Dad?" Kandi asked mockingly.

"How about my house?"

"OK," Kandi said with some reticence. She was suspicious about the sudden change of plans. *Why was he so anxious to get home?* She quickly dismissed her concern.

Troy hit the gas when he merged onto the interstate. Sixty five, seventy-five, eighty miles an hour. He tossed a Red Hot Chili Peppers CD into the player. For a while they didn't talk. They just enjoyed the sights accompanied by the driving rhythm of the music. Kandi cast aside any concern, thinking to herself, *I never would have guessed a couple of weeks ago back in Amarillo that I would be cruising Indianapolis in a Camero with the senior guard of the basketball team.* Adrenaline pumped through her veins. She snatched his sunglasses that hung from the rearview mirror.

In a matter of minutes they arrived in the posh neighborhood of Englewood. Kandi was amazed by the huge houses, the three- and four-car garages, the beautifully landscaped jogging trail that wove it's way around the wooded subdivision. She tried to mask her surprise, but she couldn't help the look on her face. *Now this is the life,* she thought to herself. Troy slowed the car down as they approached the large two-story red brick house where he lived with his parents. Troy, an only child, enjoyed his life as the son of two very successful professionals. Sandra worked as a marketing executive for the Indiana Pacers. Gordon brought home more than his share of the bacon as a regional manager of Mutual Finance International. The house, with all its amenities, served as an outward symbol of their successful track record in the business world.

Kandi followed Troy to the back door of the house and wait-

ed while he unlocked the door. It was hard for Kandi to imagine a more perfect home. She tried to hide her surprise at the
undeniable wealth of Troy's family, which was made obvious by
the pristine home. She smiled and tried acting casual.

As they walked in, Troy turned her around and kissed her.
He embraced her for a few moments when she felt a slight
sense of self-consciousness.

"Where's your mom?" she asked quietly.

"Kandi," he said with a puzzled 'as if' look, "it's only 3:45.
They won't be home until later."

Kandi felt a twinge of hesitance. Something didn't feel
right. She felt like she had been drawn into a trap. First the ride
home. Then the invitation to go get some ice cream and then
a quick change of plans directly to his home where they'd be
alone for an hour if not longer. But she resisted the thought.
This is Troy. He's one of the nicest guys I've ever met. Troy kissed
her again with more power and freedom. She turned from him
and nervously blurted out, "So are you going to give me the
grand tour?"

"I'd love to give you the grand tour," Troy said with a
light laugh.

I'm so stupid! she thought. *That didn't sound good at all. He
may have read something into that.*

But from all indications, the tour was on. He showed her
the kitchen, his mom and dad's room, the game room, and the
back porch. At each room Kandi would struggle to make conversation, trying to waste as much time as possible before she
was saved by the arrival of Troy's parent's. She had no doubt
now that Troy would steer her in a direction she didn't want to

go. Troy moved quickly, slyly. She wanted desperately for Troy
to be a real man, to respect and honor her, but she feared the
worst. When they got to the covered back porch Kandi sat
down on the swing. She found a sense of protection in the
open air. He sat down next to her and held her hand. She felt
uncomfortable being alone in the house with him. He took her
hand on the swing as they watched the clouds break and the
sun settle between the trees.

They talked on the swing for a few minutes. "It's getting
cold out here," Troy said finally.

"It feels good," Kandi said.

"Wouldn't you like to see the rest of the house?" Troy
asked. He caressed her arm and looked into her eyes.

"What are you thinking?" Kandi asked.

"I'm thinking that . . . you're beautiful."

Her hungry heart melted and her inhibitions vanished. He
kissed her tenderly.

"Come on," Troy said. "Let's go inside before you
catch cold."

For some odd reason she felt safer now. Troy sounded just
like her father did when he was sober and well.

They walked through the door and went down the hall. He
showed her the home office and his bedroom. They talked
casually, but the conversation quickly died, and they were both
left staring into each other's eyes. His eyes cut over to the bed
and then back to her. It was very obvious now what he wanted,
although no words were spoken. He kissed her again. But this
time his kiss was stronger, with a sense of power and purpose.
He pressed her back against the wall of the room as his hand

slid down to the second button of her shirt. She pushed him away, whispering, "No, Troy."

"Why not?"

"It just doesn't feel right to—"

"It will, I promise," He tried to kiss her again, but she turned her head.

He looked at her in frustration, then pounded his fist on the wall a few inches from her face. She walked away from him, her chin quivering. This was exactly what she had wanted to avoid. At that moment she felt more like an object than a person, a mere utility of someone's personal fantasy. She felt a dark cloud of shame. She scanned across the events of the past few days, trying to decide what she did that provoked him.

"I'm sorry," he said coldly. "I just thought you felt the same way I do."

"About what?"

"About our relationship."

"I think I do," Kandi said. "But I'm not ready to get that close right now. I've been through a whole lot in the past couple of weeks, and I'm just so unsure about my feelings. I just didn't want to do something I'd regret. I don't know. Everything's moving so fast. Will you be patient with me?"

He looked down on the floor and then his eyes moved up to her face. They stared at each other for an endless moment. Kandi's heart pounded as his whole demeanor changed. He walked slowly and wrapped his arms around her waist. He kissed her again, but this time Kandi's response was cold and unresponsive. He opened his eyes and stared at her. He pointed his finger at her. "You led me on," he said accusingly.

He scorned her with obscene words and a low growl in his
voice. She could no longer hold back the tears.

"Please Troy, don't do this. Why are you doing this to me?"

He shoved her onto the bed.

"No!"

"Oh, come on!" he laughed coldly.

He pressed her shoulders down.

Kandi sobbed and pleaded for him to stop as he gripped
the shoulders of her shirt. Finally her pleading turned to rage.
She freed her right arm, drew it back, and delivered a blow to
his temple with enough force to knock him off her. She
glanced down at him for a moment, a bit shocked that she had
the strength to defend herself so well. But she didn't waste any
time. She ran to the front door, unlocked it, and burst out, still
shaking in fright. The moment she opened the door a terrible
high-pitched alarm filled the air.

Troy caught up with her just a few feet from the door and
angrily grabbed her arm. She was no longer concerned about
who heard her. She was furious!

"Get your hands off me!" Kandi screamed.

"You'd better settle down, or you're going to have to walk
all the way back to your little apartment."

The condescending tone in his voice infuriated her
even more.

"Let go of me. NOW!"

Troy looked up and saw the mail carrier, who stared in
total disbelief.

"Hey, kid. I think she wants you to let her go."

"I'm cool," he said calmly, "Just a little argument with my girlfriend."

The mail carrier shook his head in disgust.

Kandi said under her breath, "I'm *not* your girlfriend."

She started walking away from Troy and the house. Troy caught up with her. "Where are you going?"

"I don't know," she said at first, then, "I'm going home."

"You're crazy. It's ten miles from here." He grabbed her arm and turned her around.

She jerked her arm out of his tight grip. "Don't touch me! Go away!"

It began to drizzle again. "What is your problem?" he growled. "I invite you over. You come onto me in the car and then you fridge out on me. What did you expect?! You knew my parents weren't home. You knew what was up. You're a mental case."

"Leave me alone," she screamed. "I promise. If you ever touch me again—"

"What? What are you going to do?" He laughed.

She turned from him and began to run. She hardly knew the way out of the neighborhood. By the time she made it to the brick entrance, the rain was coming down in sheets. She was drenched, cold, and sobbing. Kandi ran down the boulevard to a convenience store, trying to clear her mind. She was humiliated. She didn't want to call her mom. She didn't even think she could explain to her where she was. Calling a cab was also out of the question, she had left her purse in Troy's car.

"Is something wrong?" the store clerk asked.

"Can I use your phone?"

"Sure."

There seemed to be no other choice. She had to call her mom. But what would she say? She felt so gullible and was afraid her mom might suspect she wasn't telling the truth about their plans. As she picked up the phone, she reached into her pocket and pulled out the piece of yellow paper with Justin's phone number. She had completely forgotten about it. Her eyes lit up. "I'll call Justin."

She was unsure about what to say, but she knew that he offered his help at anytime. She dialed the number. A young child answered. *Must have a younger brother,* Kandi thought.

"Hello."

"Hi. May I speak to Justin."

"Mommy?"

"No. This is a friend."

"Who is this?"

"Kandi."

"Candy? You got some candy?"

Even in the midst of all the stress she couldn't help but smile. She heard Justin walking over to the phone, scolding his brother in whispered voice.

"How many times do I have to tell you not to answer the phone." He took the phone from him. "Sorry about that."

"Hi . . . uh Justin?"

"Hey."

"This is Kandi."

"Hi, Kandi. How's it going?"

"Not so good. I need a little help. I'm stranded."

"You are? Where? Did your car break down or something?"

"It's a really long story."

"No prob. You need a ride home?"

She looked at herself in the reflection of the store window. She looked like a haggard wet cat, making her even more embarrassed by the whole scene.

"I do, but you don't have to pick me up."

"Of course I do. Where are you?"

"You're taking care of your brother."

"Just for a few minutes. My mom, uh, I mean my step-mom's going to walk in any minute now, he said feeling a little awkward at explaining his family configuration to her. He never thought of her as a stepmom. She was the only mom he had ever known. "But I could put him in the car seat and pick you up in no time."

"If you could just call Melissa."

"Her mom won't let her drive."

"Do you know of anyone else who could come by?"

"I insist."

"No, Justin, don't insist," she said assertively.

"Where are you, Kandi?"

She hesitated. "I'm at a 7-ll near . . ." She stopped for a moment, knowing the conclusions he may draw from the location. "Near Englewood Estates."

There was silence on the other end of the phone.

"Does this have anything to do with Troy?"

"Justin!" *I am so sick of guys!* she thought.

"Sorry. My fault. Me and my big nose. Look, I just heard Mom pull in. I'll be there in about fifteen minutes."

"Justin, I—"

"Don't leave with somebody else, or I'll call missing persons and have your picture stamped on every milk carton in the county."

He made her smile, but the moment she hung up the phone, her mind returned to the events of the past hour and what she would tell her mother when she got home.

Kandi stayed in her room that night, aching. She was alone
again. What could she do? Where could she turn to fill this void?
She wanted to reach out to someone bigger than she was. She
wanted someone to hold her and wipe the tears away. She wanted so desperately to be cherished and cared for. All she felt that
night was rejection. She picked up the phone. She wanted to call
someone who knew her longer than one week. The only person
within five hundred miles that fit the criteria was her mom, and
she just couldn't talk to her about what had happened and what
she felt. Finally she decided to call Blake. Blake and Kandi had
gone out for three months, but after they realized that a move
was inevitable, they had decided to discontinue the relationship.
Blake was a great guy but long distance relationships, they both
agreed, were a drag. But Kandi still thought of him often and
wrote him that very first night she spent in Indy. She pulled the
letter up on her computer screen and read it again.

Dear Blake,

Here I am. My first night in Indianapolis. The flight was fine and I'm beginning to get unpacked. Taking a break now and I'm thinking of you. Blake, I really do miss seeing you already. I'm sure I'll get adjusted and you will too, but I wish we were together again, exploring the canyons with our friends from Tascosa High. We sure had a lot of fun back then. I guess the old saying is true, "You don't know exactly what you have until it's over." I know we agreed that it'd be best for us not to even think *about staying together, but I hope we'll still be close. I hope you'll write me soon or even call. I gave you my new number the other day but just in case— 317-555-3690.*

I'm missing you more than I expected. Tell everybody hi for me. I'll let you know how Summit High works out. Please call!

Love,
Kandi

She had mailed the letter several days ago. She expected to hear from him, but she'd been out of the house so much that she assumed she had missed the call. She was so needy for affirmation, for someone to listen to her intently and remind her of who she really was. Blake wasn't the popular type like Troy. He was deeper and more sincere in character and action. She had wondered what Blake would say to her once she told him about Troy's attack. She imagined that he'd become furious. She wanted to hear his outrage. She picked up the phone and dialed the area code and part of the number three times before hanging up. Finally, she worked up enough courage to complete the call.

━ ❦ ➛

After three rings a female voice answered the phone. "Hello?"

"Yes, is this the Calloway residence?"

"Yes." The voice on the other end of the line sounded familiar, but she couldn't place it.

"Can I speak to Blake?"

"Sure. Who's this?"

"It's Kandi."

There was silence for a long moment as if the voice was in sudden shock. The voice continued—slightly enthusiastic yet also uncomfortable. "Oh . . . Hi Kandi! It's Rebecca."

Kandi's heart sunk even further. Rebecca was one of Kandi's friends. They had been on double dates together on several occasions. Kandi tried to talk herself out of all the negative feelings she was having at that moment, but she could not do it. She thought, *They are friends. Have been for years. Snap out of it. They might not even be dating, but even if they are, what right do you have to feel bad about this? You're out of the picture. He's free.* Still, all the logic she could muster would not relieve the emotional burden that clung to her spirit.

Kandi tried to match Rebecca's forced enthusiasm, "Hey! How are you?"

"Fine. I'm doing good. You sound like you're right here in town. Are you?"

"I'm in Indiana. I wish I was there."

"Bet you do." There was another uncomfortable pause. "I guess you want to talk to Blake. Uh . . . He's right here—"

"No really. I don't . . . I mean . . . I can call back later—"

"Kandi . . . He's right here."

Kandi could hear the muffling of the phone and faint whispers on the other end. Her heart pounded and her face felt warm with embarrassment.

"Hey, Kandi," Blake said.

"Hi. I just wanted to call and—"

"I'm glad you did. How's Indiana?"

She thought about telling him the truth, but she was hurting so badly that she was afraid she might cry and cause Blake to feel responsible. Now she just wanted to hang up the phone. *I have no right to feel this way!* She thought. But she couldn't help the hurt. She couldn't mask it. In a split second she made the decision to lie. "Indiana's great." Another wretched moment of silence then, "But I sure miss ya'll."

"We miss you too."

"Did you get my letter?"

"Sure did. In fact I was going to call you but, you know me, I lost your number."

"I put it in the letter."

"Right."

More silence.

Kandi breathed deeply and paced the floor as she held the phone and twisted the cord around her index finger. "Listen, I'll call back later—"

"I'll call you tonight, Kandi."

"Will you? That'd be great. I wanted to tell you what's been going on here." She felt that this was enough bait to heighten his curiosity. She couldn't believe that she was being so manipulative as to obligate him to call her. She felt worthless and simple, like a child vying for her father's attention.

She hung up the phone and wept. The walls seemed to close in around her. She felt trapped, held hostage by her own loneliness. As she had done many times before, she retreated to her journal and wrote out her struggle in poetic form:

> *Can you imagine how it hurts?*
> *A loneliness that sears right,*
> *leaving nothing but wrong*
> *prevailing in a world of doubt.*
> *It weaves intentions into futile attempts at sanity.*
> *It longs throatlessly for a breath of faith,*
> *but never seems content to believe.*
> *There's no believing in hope.*
> *Why hope in futility?*
> *It brings only vain giving,*
> *and sings of imaginary princes and toads.*
> *The seasons change, having no need of companionship.*
> *How I wish I were a tree or a librarian!*
> *How many times have I wanted not to want*
> *and wished not to wish!*
> *Ending this cycle of silence.*
> *How I hate the seasons,*
> *for they remind me of what I am not . . .*
> *For I linger each lonely night in sullen repose,*
> *desiring to enter the heart and soul of another.*
> *But my world is still empty.*
> *My dream still hollow . . .*

She closed her journal and tried to escape into a novel that was on her bedside table. She read and thought and stared at the phone for what seemed an eternity. Every now and then she prayed to a God she did not know. In other moments her mind returned to a better day, before the abuse and fear, which had been dutifully served to her and her mother by a drunken, desperate father. She remembered her childhood, her dreams, and her hopes. She thought of all these things and waited. But Blake never called.

10

Although Summit High was a large school, it boasted of a grapevine so sleek and aerodynamic that it could spread a rumor from the cafeteria to the west wing in less than sixty seconds. It could take the slightest morsel of information and disseminate it to all networks of cliques and social groups in no time. Information traveled through locker rooms, into computers, on bathroom walls, and through hallways. Kandi learned this the hard way. Her morning following the sleepless night started off fine. She was fatigued but hanging in there. But as the hours progressed, she watched her reputation fade from an attractive, friendly new student at Summit to the new villainous tease.

She started perceiving the evolution as she walked through the halls between first and second period. As she passed two groups of girls, they stopped their frantic talking and began glaring the moment she walked by.

Is this really happening? Are they really staring at me or am I just feeling a little self-conscious, she asked herself. If looks could kill, Kandi would have been embalmed sometime between third period and lunch. Those types of glares were reserved only for "bad girls." Her suspicions were confirmed when she went to her locker and saw defaming vulgarities written on it in bright red lipstick. She was fuming. She knew what this was all about. Troy was letting her know of his disapproval by alienating her from the entire student body.

As the warning bell rang for the end of her lunch shift, Melissa filled her in on the news. "I don't have much time, but let me put it this way. Word has it that you seduced Troy. You had sex with him and then you dropped him cold."

Kandi stood in stunned disbelief and then erupted in volcanic anger. "What?! You've got to be kidding! That's a lie!"

"Kandi, I didn't say it was true. I'm just telling you what I'm hearing."

"And you just sat there and listened to that junk?"

"What was I supposed to do? I didn't even know what they were talking about. I didn't hear your side of the story."

"*My* side of the story? How dare you! Don't you know me! Do you think that I'd—"

Melissa interrupted tearfully, "That's the whole point, Kandi. I *don't* know you. We just met last week."

Kandi looked away as her eyes moistened. She felt as if she couldn't defend herself. She knew that her reputation had been destroyed before it had a chance to develop. She was beyond disappointment. She was enraged and vowed not to talk to anyone for the rest of the day, and she didn't until after school when she happened to see Troy walking down an empty hall, smoking a cigarette. He acted like she was invisible as they almost crossed each other.

"Troy."

"Yeah," he said as he flicked the butt of the cigarette on the hall floor and stepped on it.

"I really can't believe this. As if yesterday afternoon wasn't enough," Kandi fumed.

"Touchy, touchy . . ." Troy said with his hands halfway in the air.

"I should have turned you into the police for attempted rape!" She continued, her voice gaining in intensity and volume.

"Shut up, chick." He said looking around, quickly checking the hall for onlookers.

"Don't call me that!"

"You wanted it and now look at you," Troy said in a hushed voice.

I wouldn't have believed it could possibly get worse, but listen to him! she thought to herself. "What are you talking about? What planet were you abducted from? I *never* wanted 'it'!"

"Listen, Kandi. You're new here. This is my house, and you'll play by my rules at Summit." His voice lowered as he got right in her face, "I've never been turned down like that before."

"Well I'd say it was about time."

Troy grabbed Kandi's arm and squeezed it hard. "Shut up!" he said, then let out a string of obscene attacks on her character. Kandi wept in pain and humiliation. Neither of them noticed Clipper who stopped at the front of the hall about fifty feet from the two. The moment Clipper saw what was happening, his instincts took over. He bolted straight for Troy's midsection like a red streak. Kandi and Troy saw him as he went airborne about eight feet from them. WHAM! Clipper, tackled the other boy with the force of an all-state linebacker. Kandi stood there in stunned disbelief and then ran away not looking back. Troy fell on his back but quickly rolled Clipper over and retaliated with a series of blows to the chin and nose and an occasional shot to the stomach. Clipper's instincts didn't accurately estimate the mismatch. Troy finally stood up, looking down at Clipper, who was writhing in pain, the wind knocked out of him, nose bleeding and lip busted. "I wouldn't try that again if I were you," Troy said smiling. "We're supposed to be on the same team." Then he kicked Clipper in the stomach for good measure and walked away.

That night Melissa called Kandi. She felt terrible about their conversation that day. "I'm sorry, Kandi. You were right. I shouldn't have listened to them. I should have defended you. We haven't known each other that long, but I trust you more than I trust Troy. I wouldn't trust Troy further than I could throw him. There's no way it could be true. You're a good person."

"Is it as bad as you made it out to be?" Kandi asked.

"Truthfully?"

"Yes. *Of course* truthfully."

"Yes. They've made a five-course meal out of what happened last night. I'm sure Troy started the whole thing. Who else? So what did happen?"

"Melissa, I don't want to get into it right now. I'm tired. I hardly slept two hours last night."

"No problem. I understand. But sooner or later you're going to have to stand up for yourself, you know? Troy's an egotistical jerk. I'm finally catching on to that. He thinks he owns the school."

"After he ruined my reputation in less than three hours today, I'd have to say that he just about does," Kandi said.

The next morning, Kandi's mom knocked on her door. Kandi had gone to bed at seven the night before and was still asleep. "Kandi?" She knocked again, louder this time. "Kandi?"

"Yeah, Mom. I'm awake."

"You had me worried, Kandi. It's 7:00 A.M. You've been asleep for twelve hours. Are you OK? Planning to go to school, aren't you?"

"I don't know. I'm fine," she lied. "Guess I'm just a little tired from all the change."

"Feel free to take a day off if you'd like," Kandi's mom offered.

"I really can't. Did you say 7:00?"

"You got it."

"I'm late."

"I can go in to work late if you want me to drop you off at the school."

"That'd be great. Thanks, Mom."

"By the way, a guy came by last night at around 8:00. Two guys in one week. I'm impressed. He wanted to talk to you but

I knew you'd probably wouldn't want me to wake you up so he wrote you a note. Justin. I think that was his name. He said that he invited you to a Bible study and wanted to give you a map. He sat in our kitchen for about thirty minutes writing you a note on the back of the map. That *really* impressed me. Seems like a nice guy. Another basketball player. Go girl!" Sylvia said in forced parental hipness. "Don't worry. I didn't read it."

She tossed the note to Kandi, who sat up and folded her legs on the bed. "I'll be ready in about thirty minutes, Mom," Kandi called out.

"I'll believe it when I see it!" Sylvia said laughingly.

Kandi opened the note and read,

Hi Kandi,

I came by hoping that I'd be able to talk to you. I really wanted to see you. I know this was a day that you'd probably like to block out of your memory. I saw Clipper after school and took him to the hospital to get his nose checked out. (By the way, he's fine.) Sometimes he acts before he thinks, but if I'd have been there, I would have probably done the same thing. I'm so sorry about how things have worked out here, but I believe in you, and we really do care about what's going on. I heard some pretty strange stories—stories that made me mad because I know that they weren't true. I wish I could convince you that I believe in you. Troy and I have known each other since we were in elementary school. He's got a big mouth and throws his weight around by lying about people who cross him. I know that you probably don't want to talk about what happened Monday, and that's fine. I just had to let you know that I'm your friend, and I've learned over the past couple of months that being a friend means believing the best of someone. That's the way I feel about you. Melissa feels the same way. I talked to her and she feels like she really blew it. I hope you'll give her a second chance. I'm glad to hear that you're getting some sleep. I hope I can sleep tonight. I'm having a hard time about the whole situation. I don't know how to say it, without sounding sappy, but what the heck . . . I'll say it anyway, I care.

> *Your friend,*
> *Justin*

P.S. On the other side of this paper there's a map to my house, where we're having the Bible study. Hope you can make it! (Don't worry. I'll try to keep Clipper from tackling people that talk to you! He's an animal, isn't he?)

To guys like Clipper, there are few things that compare with Indiana high school basketball in March. Summit High could clench a berth in the state playoffs. They had two games left on the schedule, and they only needed one win. First, they faced a below-average team—Woodlawn High School. Then they would face their cross town rival—Western High. Western had won two state championships in recent years and consistently remained on the *USA Today* Top 25 poll of high school basketball teams across the country. They were a true basketball dynasty. The coach of Western actually left a college position for a chance to coach this great team. They were dominating.

The first game took place Saturday night at Woodlawn. With the help of a packed house of partisan Woodlawn Pioneers, Summit players found themselves in a close game. Tupper was furious with the team's performance. They were playing way below their potential and in all respects, this was a must-win.

When one of the Summit's starting players continued to perform poorly, Tupper went for his secret weapon. The mighty elbow himself: Clipper Hayes. Clipper's family and friends cheered loudly when they heard his name called. They knew better than anyone that destiny had smiled on a lifetime dream. He really didn't expect to play, but Tupper was willing to take a chance and give him a few seconds toward the end of the first half. His defensive abilities seemed to intensify under pressure. Defensively, he shined during the two minutes he played. Summit was sparked by his dive into the stands to save the ball and a hard fought rebound.

But in the second half when Coach Tupper put him in, Clipper missed two huge free throws with less than two minutes to go.

Troy shook his head and glared at the coach. *Why did he have their worst foul shooter in the game in the final seconds?* he asked himself in frustration.

The coach's call paid off, however, when Clipper made another athletic rebound with thirty seconds left in the game. Though hundreds of people were packed in the small gym, Clipper could hear his dad shout, "YES!" Clipper's heart pounded as he gripped the ball. It felt as heavy as metal. Summit was down by a point, and Clipper couldn't throw it to Troy soon enough. The pass was perfect and the weight of the world was lifted off of his shoulder. He didn't want to be fouled with the ball and be forced to shoot the free throws, not with the season on the line. His confidence was blown from his last trip to the line.

Troy took the ball and spotted Justin making a break for the goal; he was open. But Troy was having a great night. He had scored a season high twenty-eight points and the moment was all his. He dribbled down the court and stopped about fifteen feet from the goal, putting up a beautiful jump shot. The moment hung in the air as they watched the ball arching toward the goal. But the ball hit the front rim and bounded off the back as the Woodlawn partisan went crazy. They were nowhere near an invitation to the state tournament, so this was the biggest game of the year for them, and they celebrated it like a state championship.

As the ball bounced to the floor and the Woodlawn Pioneers began their celebration, it was as if Summit was watching their whole season go down the drain. This had been their golden opportunity to go to state, and they had blown it. Now they had to wish for a certified sports miracle against highly favored Western High next week.

Tupper was almost too disappointed to go into the locker room to talk with his players. The room was hot, humid, and quiet as the boys sat in a stunned circle. Only Tad's whistling a rendition of Queen's "We Will Rock You" broke the silence. Everyone just stared at him, puzzled by his strange expression of grief. They all thought, *Why is he whistling? We just got upset by a losing team and what does Tad do? He whistles the other team's fight song!*

"Would you shut that up?" Troy demanded of his friend.

"Shut what up? I didn't say anything."

"Oh, get out! We just lost our best chance at State and you're whistling."

"So what? Do you think it's gonna do any good to sit around cryin' about it?" Tad replied and then began a sarcastic pep talk, "Do you think Babe Ruth cried when he struck out? Did George Washington cry when he got in trouble for chop-pin' down the cherry tree?

"SHUT UP!" Jared screamed.

"Touchy, touchy," Tad remarked.

"Troy, why didn't you pass it?" Justin asked. "You looked straight at me on that last play. I was five feet further down the court than anybody else. I could have laid it in, no problem."

"Justin, how many points did you score?" Troy asked as if cross-examining a criminal.

"I don't know but—"

"You know how many. You scored three. Do you know how many points *I* scored? Huh? I scored 28. Now tell me what you would have done."

"If I were you, I would've trusted the open man to make the easy layup."

"But you're *not* me. We wouldn't be having this discussion if Clipper would give us all a break and hit a free throw in the clutch!"

Clipper looked away and then bowed his head in silent agreement.

Justin got right in Troy's face and grabbed a hand full of the number on his jersey and pushed him against the locker. Justin's old ways came back to him easily, "You lay off him. Where do you get off blaming Clipper."

"Whoa! Mr. Rogers goes ballistic," Troy mocked.

"Why don't you eat your own crow? You lost the game, man. Not Clipper."

Troy pushed Justin out of his face with both hands, "Go ahead. You want a piece of me? Here's your chance."

"It would be my pleasure," Justin said under his breath. But he caught himself. In that moment he realized how hypocritical it was for him to publicly claim Jesus as Savior and then knock his teammate's teeth out. He loosened his grip and turned away.

"What happened Justin? You really *are* a wimp," Troy said. "Don't touch me again unless you plan to back it up, boy."

Not another word was spoken in the locker room outside of Lunsford's and Tupper's post-game briefing. They tried to get the team focused on the final game of the season, but it was obvious to everyone in the room that morale had never been this low.

When Summit's team loaded onto the bus, Troy taunted Justin again in a soft voice, "I heard you were a real hero the other day with Kandi. Bet you have the hots for the girl. You can have her. I got her blood pumping the other night. I don't know what she told you, but believe me, she wanted it. But anyway . . . she ain't my type."

Justin looked straight ahead, knowing that Troy was trying to provoke something nasty that might get him expelled. Justin's heart was racing. It took everything in him not to give Troy what he had coming. He took in a breath of air. Let it out slowly and prayed silently, *Lord, please keep me from my old ways. Spare me from this compulsion to slam my fist down his throat*. He turned around to Troy, who was sitting in the seat behind him and said as calmly as he could, "Troy, I know you're upset about the game and you're bummed out that you

wasted your time on a girl that happened to have some
principles, but I'm warning you to shut up about Kandi."

"Ooooo. Do I sense jealously?"

"Nope. I'm not going to tell you what you're sensing right
now. Please. Give it a rest. And be advised—"

"What are you, a lawyer?" Troy asked.

"Be advised. Don't talk to her. Don't touch her. Or I'll be
coming for you."

Was it right for him to draw a line and make such a
promise? Justin didn't know.

"So he picked you up?" Melissa asked as she drove
Kandi home.

"I didn't have any choice. I wasn't going to call my mom."

"You could have called me."

"I didn't have your number."

"You like him, don't you?" Melissa asked.

"I can't believe you're asking me that! I tell you that I
almost got raped by the senior class favorite of Summit High,
and you think I called Justin because I wanted a date."

"I didn't say you wanted a date. I just—"

"Yes, you did," Kandi said.

"I just said that you could like him."

"Right then, I could have cared less about . . . about Chris
O'Donnell. Troy was a jerk."

Melissa smiled sarcastically, "Hmm . . . Troy's a jerk. Troy's
a guy. Therefore all guys are jerks. I think you were
oversimplifying."

"It was pretty humiliating. I was soaked to the bone. I looked like I'd been washed up in some gutter."

"Did you tell him what happened?"

"I tried to act normal about the whole thing, but the situation was far from normal. I couldn't even come up with a decent lie. My eyes were red from crying, my hair was dripping. I was shivering."

"So what did he say when he picked you up?"

"That part was really strange. He didn't say all that much. He asked me where I lived and about five minutes later he asked if I was going to be all right and then we were home. He pulled up to the apartment and asked if I wanted him to walk me to the apartment and I told him, no thanks. He didn't even push me about the Bible study. I could tell he was just angry."

"At you?"

"No, Melissa! He was mad at Troy. It was like he knew what had happened."

"If you haven't noticed, Kandi, Troy and Justin aren't exactly pals."

"What happened?" Kandi asked.

"They used to hang out a lot together. Justin always looked up to Troy. They partied together and were really tight, but then Justin started on this Jesus kick, which was a real turnoff to Troy. I don't understand the whole deal with Justin. He's a sweet guy, but he takes all the religion stuff way too far. I mean, I'm a Christian too. In fact, Justin and I go to the same church, but he's too freaky for me. He carries this little *New Testament* around with him and he reads it. Can you believe it? When he's just hanging out, he reads that green *New Testament*. He dog-ears it like he was reading a John Grisham novel. What's that all about? Sheesh!"

Kandi just looked puzzled after this long discourse on rivals and theology. Melissa hardly stopped for a breath, and Kandi was a little surprised when she did. They looked at each other and then looked straight ahead at the road.

"So did he ask you out?" Melissa asked as she folded a stick of gum into her mouth.

"Nope. Melissa, let me say this again just like I told you on the way to the game. I am way too shaky about guys to even care about dating, even if I had an armed guard escort and stun gun with me the whole time."

Melissa burst out laughing. It almost frightened Kandi. There were some things that went straight over Melissa's head and other things that were extraordinarily funny to her. The uncanny thing was that no one could ever judge what reaction would come when. "You're back to that 'all guys are jerks' thing again," Melissa said, laughing.

"I guess I am."

"So are you going?" Melissa asked.

"Going?"

"I mean to the Bible study?"

Kandi paused for a moment thinking. "I guess I am."

"Don't let the Bible bug bite you too."

"I'll do my best," Kandi replied.

Melissa pulled into the apartment.

"How 'bout you?" Kandi asked.

"No thanks. Sunday morning does me just fine."

"Oh come on! The only people I know that'll be there are Justin and Clipper."

"Maybe. But please don't ask me tonight." She stopped the car and Kandi got out. "Give me some time to make up a good excuse."

"You're impossible, Melissa."

"But I was the first one to speak to you, so you're stuck with me. Those are the rules, girl." She laughed at her own cleverness and wheeled away.

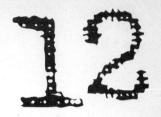

At 9:00 on Sunday morning, Troy was hunkered down in bed trying to sleep off his depression from the game. His mom banged on the door, "Troy, telephone."

"Who is it?"

"I don't know. It's a girl," she said as Troy shuffled through his dresser to find gym shorts and a T-shirt. "I knew that would wake you up," she said jokingly.

"Gimme a second," Troy said, a bit annoyed.

"Hurry up, Troy. She's not at the door. She's on the phone."

"If you'd let me have my extra phone line, you wouldn't have this problem," Troy said as he opened the door.

"If you wouldn't call 1-900 numbers, you would have the extra line," Troy's mom said as she cupped her hand over the mouth piece.

Troy grabbed the phone and rolled his eyes at his mom. His mom just stared at him and smiled.

"What are you doing?" He whispered, "Go away. Shoo!"

"Why is it that I'm always the last one to know about these girls?"

"Please."

His mom relented and headed back toward the kitchen.

"Hello."

"Uh . . . Troy. This is Kamden."

"Kamden?"

"I know you probably don't know me that well. I'm a freshman. I was at that party a few months ago. The one that you crashed at Debbie's house."

"Debbie McAllister's house?" Troy asked.

"Debbie *Archer's* house."

"Right, so what's this all about?"

"Well—"

"Hey I remember now. You're the blonde haired JV cheerleader, aren't you?"

"Right."

Troy continued the conversation with new interest and curiosity. "How's everything?" he said with stiff congeniality. He had no idea why this girl was calling him. But he could only hope.

"Can I see you sometime, Troy? I want to talk to you."

"Sure. You pick the place and I'm there."

"How about today? This afternoon."

"Is this some kind of prank?" Troy asked.

Kamden didn't miss a beat. "No. It's not a prank. I just want to talk to you."

"Sure. I'm open. How about at one. Where would you like to meet?"

"Can you meet me at the Medical Center Park by the pond?" Kamden asked.

"Sure," Troy replied.

"I'll see you there."

"Thanks, Troy."

"Kamden? What's this all about?"

There was a moment of silence on the other side of the phone. "I just want to see you."

"OK. I'm all yours," Troy said with a smile. He hung up the phone, wondering why this freshman who had never talked to him before called him now.

That afternoon, Troy made his way to the Medical Center Park. The rains that blanketed most of central Indiana were no more. It was a beautiful day outside. As he drove across town, he watched as the churches emptied and cars headed home from worship and mass. Troy went to church sporadically, mainly for social reasons. His parents had stopped going years ago. He vaguely remembered going with them when he was four or five, but as they became more and more successful in the business world, church had faded into the background. Troy's dad had a bad experience with the church leadership. He saw inconsistency in ethics and a general disregard for people in the churches he'd attended, and, as a result, considered it pointless. For his parents, Sunday morning was a time to sleep in, drink coffee, and watch CNN. Nothing more.

After circling the park, he found Kamden sitting on a bench looking straight ahead, focusing on nothing. Troy could sense her preoccupation the moment their eyes met. She forced a smile, "Hey, Troy."

"Hey, mystery girl." He casually eased his arm around her shoulders, testing the waters. Kamden countered by standing up and walking away.

"OK, you're not moved by my charm."

"Nope."

"So, you called the meeting. What's up?"

"It's about Susan."

"Susan?"

"Susan Stedham."

"That's the girl who died in an accident a few days ago."

"Right."

"What was her deal? Word has it that she slammed into the tree to kill herself. Pulled a 'Cobain.'"

"She was a good friend of mine," Kamden said quietly. "Probably my best friend. She was a couple years older than me so I really looked up to her."

Silence. Troy's demeanor changed. "I'm sorry. I didn't know you were close to her."

"Do you remember much about that party at Debbie's house?" Kamden asked.

"That was last summer, and I wasn't as straight as I am now. To tell you the truth, I remember going, but I was pretty smashed by the time I got there."

"Don't you remember being with Susan?"

Troy looked away, exhaled and began to back away from her. "I really don't like where this conversation is going."

"Hear me out. You were with her. You danced for about

half an hour with her. Debbie's parents were gone, and we were all over that house. Susan was so stoked about being with you. It was like forbidden fruit. You don't exactly run around with our kind."

"Your kind?" Troy questioned.

"Our group. You know what I mean. She couldn't stop talking about you. I remember that I didn't see you or Susan for at least an hour, and by that time, it must have been 11:30 or 12."

"So what?"

"You know what I mean, Troy."

"No, I don't," Troy said defensively.

"Troy, she told me all about it. She wasn't totally pure. She had a boyfriend through the ninth and tenth grade, and she said they got way too involved physically, and it ruined their relationship, but she never had sex with someone right after they first met."

"This conversation is boring me. Do you believe everything that people tell you?" Troy said.

"Are you saying that she was just lying to me? Why would she lie?"

"I'm saying I don't remember what happened that night. But I think I would remember that," Troy replied. He began to walk ahead of Kamden.

Kamden turned him around. She was in tears. "This isn't fun for me either, Troy."

Troy tightened his jaw and raised his voice, "Then why are you doing it? Are you trying to do a documentary on my exploits? I don't think A&E would be interested. Are you trying to say that I had anything to do with Susan wrapping her car

around a tree the other night? You've got some kind of imagination, Kamden. That was over six months ago. I never spoke
to her again."

"That's right! Why didn't you? You just used her up like
something temporary . . . something disposable."

"I told you I WAS SMASHED!" Troy shouted inches from
her face.

Joggers passed by trying to act as if they couldn't hear.
Perhaps embarrassed by what looked to be a humiliating spat
between a couple.

"There's something you need to know," Kamden said.

"OK. Finally. Tell me something, *anything* that I need
to know."

"Susan had the HIV virus."

Troy stared a hole right through her head.

With no response from Troy, Kamden said it again.

"Susan had the virus."

"How long have you known this?" Troy demanded harshly.

"I found out about it the same time she did," Kamden said.

Troy stood still, physically shaken by what he had heard.
He felt lightheaded and a little nauseated.

"See, she took it really hard. The news tore her in half. I
mean, she lived for a chance to be a leader. She spent lots of
time working in the D.A.R.E. program. And she had just met a
guy from Indiana State—Cal. Their relationship was so good.
He was great for her. Really level-headed. . . ."

"Evidently this Cal guy wasn't as clean as you two thought."

"They never slept together."

"How do you know?" Troy asked defensively.

"I just know! OK?" Kamden shouted back to him.

"How'd she find out about the HIV?"

"She had done a lot of research about cancer treatment. She was really into speech and debate. Anyway, she was preparing a speech for a tournament on being a bone marrow donor, and she wanted to register herself, which required a blood test. I went with her a couple of days later. We had just gotten off from school. She said she wanted to pick up the paperwork. I went into the clinic with her and when they saw that we were there, the doctor called Susan into one of the consultation rooms."

Kamden sat down on another bench and Troy joined her saying nothing. Kamden continued with her emotions barely under the surface, "I sort of knew something was up. She came out and she looked devastated. When we got into the car, she lost it. And about what I had no idea. Then she told me. We stayed in that parking lot for at least an hour. She had hope when we were driving home that maybe this whole thing had some purpose. She was going to tell her mom and dad that night, then she was going to go completely public with it at school. She was going to spend the rest of her life fighting for research and public awareness. And she could have done it too."

Troy sat there stunned at what he was hearing. Kamden paused for a few seconds and then went on, "About 11:00 Sunday night she called me and told me she just E-mailed me and that it was really important that I retrieve it before I went to bed."

"What did it say?" Troy asked.

She pulled out a folded note from her back pocket and handed it to Troy.

Dearest Kamden,

I beg you to forgive me for what I'm about to do. I hate that you've been caught up in this mess. Tonight I'm going for a ride from which I will never return. I think you can understand why. My parents think I'm a virgin. Cal thinks that I'm a virgin. I've humiliated myself, and I can't go on like this. It would hurt too many people. I've seen people die of AIDS before. I've seen their courage. But I can't stand the thought of this virus reducing me to skin and bones. I can't face my parents and tell them I'm HIV positive. I can't go through with it. I'm already weary of it all. I'm weary of life. It's hard to believe that one night last summer could bring so much pain. No one should know about this except you and Troy. Tonight I'll lose control of my car and hopefully no one will see or suspect that I did this intentionally. No one must. I knew it would be too easy for you to put the pieces together. Hopefully the doctors will respect my right to privacy, also. It's very important to me that I take this secret to the grave with me. How I wish that you weren't there when I found out. I could have spared you the suffering of knowing that I did this to myself. You see, there are some things that are more precious to me than life itself. One of those is the legacy I leave behind. I know that this is a terrible act, but I see it as my only way out. There's no hope. I love you, my friend.

S.S.

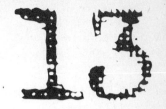

Coach Tupper called a practice for Monday afternoon. Usually this was a free day, but after the team's lackluster performance Saturday night, Tupper and Lundsford decided to set a fire under them.

"The team you played Saturday night was worse than last year's squad that you beat by twenty-some-odd points!" Tupper looked like a drill sergeant. The veins in his neck protruded with every syllable that exploded from his mouth. "What's the matter with you guys? You acted like this was some kind of square dance."

Clipper fought with every bit of mental toughness not to crack up. When Tupper was mad, he said some pretty kooky things. Clipper could only imagine the players dressed in cowboy boots and basketball shorts. *Swing yer partner round and round. Get rebound and do-si-do.*

"Clipper! What the heck are you smiling about? You think

this is funny, don't you? Well let me tell you something. I put you on the team, and I can take you off the team."

Clipper's heart raced. *Why do I have this crazy imagination! Stay focused!* he thought to himself.

Coach Tupper kicked the rolling ball back and everyone stood at attention. "Clipper! Drop down and give me 100 push-ups." Clipper's eyes expanded to saucer proportion. Coach Lunsford jerked his head over to Tupper, as Tupper realized what he had just demanded. "OK, maybe . . . fifty . . . twenty-five . . . Oh," he said in frustration, "Just start and I'll tell you when to quit," Tupper said and then continued the sermon. "Saturday night will not, I repeat, NOT happen again. If you lose, it won't be because you loaf all over the court like you did SATURDAY NIGHT. It won't be that you were flat footed when the ball hit the floor, LIKE SATURDAY NIGHT. It won't be because you weren't playing like a bunch of prima donnas LIKE SATURDAY NIGHT!"

No one was prepared for the volume, force, and total all-out veracity that would spew from the mouth of this veteran head coach: "NO ONE'S GONNA HUMILIATE ME OR THEM-SELVES LIKE THAT AGAIN!"

Clipper thought, *This man needs serious counseling*.

Tupper continued his coach's fit for another two or three minutes. Finally, he took a deep breath and looked around. He appeared puzzled with his hands on his hips and his brow furrowed. "Where's Clipper?" The players looked at each other wondering who would refresh his memory.

"He's behind you doing push-ups," Lunsford said calmly.

"Right. Right. GET OFF YOUR NOSE, CLIPPER!!"

Clipper jumped to his feet surprised he had done only four push-ups.

The practice made Saturday's game look like tennis. They crashed the boards for every rebound. Two or three times pushing matches and threats broke out. Out of frustration, fear, and desperation, Justin watched the clock on the wall with distinct interest. In a few minutes around twenty students would be welcomed into his home for a Bible study. Justin sacrificed his body and his time, but his thoughts were drawn to the question—would Kandi be there?

After the practice, Justin raced home. When he got there, several students waited for him. Slightly embarrassed by his appearance, he greeted everyone, then darted for the shower. When he returned to the living room, clothed and in his right mind, he couldn't believe it. He had slightly underestimated how many students would come.

He navigated his way across the crowded room to the kitchen. His stepmom glared at him and he knew that this ultimate organizational genius would be a little uneasy about the situation.

"Thirty-five," she said with the personality of Rod Serling, "Thirty-five kids. You said fifteen or twenty?"

"That's really all I thought would come."

"What did you tell them?"

"I just invited them to come to a Bible study on sex."

Justin looked around for Kandi, but he didn't see her. But as everyone found a seat on the floor or the furniture, he saw her sitting in the corner of the room by herself. He made his way over to her.

"Hey! Thanks for coming. Sorry I was so late; we had a last-minute practice. How'd you get here?"

"I had my mom drop me off. We just have one car and she—"

"Do you need a ride back after this is over?"

She thought for a moment, "Mom was going to come by and—"

"I don't mind," Justin interrupted.

Still hesitant because of the experience with Troy, she didn't answer right away. "I was just going to call Mom. I mean, you're already home and—"

"She's already home too. Give her a break. I'm a safe driver, and I promise I won't bite."

She smiled.

"Did I bite you the other day when I picked you up from your stroll in the rain?" Kandi shook her head and he continued, "See? There you go. I have a history of driving without biting."

She laughed, "You are nuts."

"Plus, if you thought I was a good driver the other day, you should see me drive when the road is dry. It's a thing of beauty."

"OK, OK," she relented.

"Great. Gotta do the host thing."

Justin stood up and cleared his throat in an overly dramatic, shut-up-and-listen-to-me way. "Hey, glad you could make it to my house tonight. We really weren't expecting this many, or else I would have had my parents build a bigger house. Due to our large size . . . uh, I mean number, I think my mom would like us to limit our soda intake to two ounces each." Several groans and two wads of paper were thrown in Justin's direction. "Just kidding. Hey watch it with the paper. You don't know my mom like I do, or you wouldn't do that. Shawn?"

Shawn stood up. He was the twenty-three-year-old youth minister at Justin's church and a great asset to the group. He wasn't your average cookie-cutter youth minister. He wore his long hair in a pony tail. This drove some of the older folks in the church crazy, but they couldn't argue with the results of his work. The youth group was still growing.

Shawn welcomed everyone and prayed. Then Shawn and Kelsey, a sophomore from Summit, played guitars and led the group in some simple, upbeat praise songs. At first Kandi felt uncomfortable. She'd never been to this kind of thing. But as they sang, she felt something deeply soothing, even healing, about the atmosphere. They sang a song called "We believe in God," and something inside her wanted to weep. She didn't know why at first. She looked at the faces of the students and felt their sense of togetherness. She felt the warmth of the group, yet she had never felt so alone in her entire life.

Perhaps because she had never seen God as a friend. To Kandi, the eyes of God had been the eyes of her father: unpredictable, unreliable, ready to blame and destroy. But within the hush of this crowded room, God was quite different. Did she believe in God? Did she need Jesus? This was beyond the "pray for us sinners in the hour of our death" religion. The Bible study leader talked about something different. This was a rela-

tionship with a real and living Being, who wanted a relationship with her in the here and now. Kandi felt a glimmer of
hope even though she was still not convinced. *A Bible study on
sex?* Kandi thought. *This should be interesting.*

It started with a little Scripture and lots of nervous laughter. Justin wondered from across the room what Kandi was
thinking about all this. His mind wandered from the discussion
to Kandi. He found himself staring at her until her eyes cut over
to him, then he glanced quickly back to Shawn or the person
who was speaking at the time. This must have happened three
or four times, so many times that he blushed. He thought, *It's
hard to be spiritual when you're gaga.* As he felt his wet hair
dripping from the recent shower onto his neck, he wondered,
*Why is it that when we meet, one of us has wet hair. Is this some
type of sign?*

After the group read Scriptures about the holiness of the
sexual relationship, the people in Scripture who were
destroyed by sex outside God's perfect plan, and those in the
Bible who were blessed by healthy sexual relationships within
marriage, the discussion led to their own lives and how these
principles rang true in Indy. Shawn asked the group, "What are
some of the benefits to having premarital sex? Are there any?
Now be honest. No one's going to be criticized for their opinion."

After all the Scriptures and several practical examples of
how premarital sex destroys, they awkwardly shifted gears and
talked about what people think is good about premarital sex.
Finally one of the seventh-grade guys in the back said timidly,
"I'd have to say, it feels good!" He quickly caught himself, "Of

course I'm just supposing that it feels good." This brought an avalanche of nervous laughter.

"That's honest! Thanks, Roger." Shawn said, "You're right, sex is awesome, there's no doubt about it."

Another guy chimed in, "But the feeling only lasts a little while, then you've got to deal with the consequences."

"Like what?" Shawn proposed.

Others chimed in quickly.

"You feel guilty."

"And overly obligated to something you're not even sure about."

"It's scary these days. You might contract AIDS or some disease."

"You're going to regret it later when you meet the person you want to spend the rest of your life with."

"It changes the whole relationship."

Finally one girl boldly began to talk about her experiences. "The relationship was going great," she said. "And neither one of us planned to do the things we did—neither one of us. But we thought we were in love. I remember our parents weren't too hot on us spending a lot of time together, and that seemed to draw us even closer. It's crazy how the mind works when you think you've met the one you want to spend the rest of your life with. After about three dates, we finally gave in. But I can tell you from experience that it didn't draw us any closer. After a while our relationship was totally . . . well . . . deflated. We were just like strangers to each other. It even destroyed our friendship." The girl wiped a tear that rolled down her face. "Well, I *still* miss the friendship. It was taken from me. It was like the sex destroyed everything that we had, and, believe me, we had a whole lot going for us before then. When I moved here, someone invited me to come to one of these Bible studies, and I accepted Christ about three weeks ago when Stephanie and Shawn prayed with me."

Warm applause echoed through the room.

Stephanie, who was sitting next to the girl, put her arm around her friend's shoulder. The girl once again wiped a tear away. "And I know that Christ has forgiven me. But I'm having a hard time forgiving myself. I wasted a precious part of myself on someone that I'll probably never see again in my life. And every time that I'm with a guy, I feel guilty—almost like I'm not clean. It's like when I go to church, Satan shoves the mistake right in front of my face."

Silence pervaded the room. The students gathered around her and prayed. Kandi sat back and watched in amazement. It was totally different from what she expected. She was expecting a lecture or a persuasive speech. Instead, she heard students speaking more honestly about life than she had ever heard before. It intrigued and yet frightened her. Could she be as open? Could she trust in God?

After the Bible study, the students hung out until Justin's mom began dropping hints that it was time to leave. The music and laughter shook the house. Several of the girls in the group introduced themselves to Kandi and exchanged phone numbers. Kandi went from being extremely skeptical to nearly euphoric about the experience.

Justin tapped her on the shoulder. "Are you ready?"

Kandi nodded her head, although she really didn't want to leave.

They walked out to Justin's car. "So . . ."

"So what?"

"What did you think?"

"I had a good time."

"I want to ask you a question, and you don't have to answer it. OK?"

She knew what was coming. "OK."

"What happened the other day?"

She really didn't want to talk about it. "I made a mistake. I trusted somebody."

"This somebody that you trusted—" Justin and Kandi both danced around the name Troy as they talked. "Did he . . . or she hurt you."

"No. We just had an argument, and I had to get out of there."

"Listen, Kandi. I know I'm a guy and you're a girl and—" Kandi laughed as Justin tried to recover from the statement of the obvious. "I'm not finished. Where was I?"

"You were defining what sex we are."

"Right. What I'm trying to say is that you probably wouldn't have called me if my phone number wasn't the only phone number in your pocket. Right?"

"Right."

"I just want you to feel like you can call on me if you ever need anything at all."

"Why?" Kandi asked.

"Why what?" Justin asked

"Why are you being so, uh . . . willing to help?"

"Basically?" he asked.

"Basically will do," she said.

"I'm a sucker for brown eyes."

She gritted her teeth and swung her small purse at him.

"Just joking. It's true, but I'm kidding!" he said as he laughed. "I don't know. Some things you just can't explain."

As Justin drove Kandi home, she feared he would try to make his move that night and ask her out on a date or even reach for her hand. She had hope that Justin was being truthful, that he really enjoyed the friendship, that he wasn't solely interested in her as a prospective girlfriend. As they traveled down the road toward Kandi's apartment, talking and enjoying the night, Kandi felt a glimmer of hope. Hope mingled with insecurity, fear, and disillusionment in the past few days, but hope nonetheless.

That night Kandi wrote in her journal in a way that she'd never written before:

God, I've never trusted you. To tell the truth, I've probably doubted that you even existed. I don't know why. I want to believe in you. Maybe that's because I need to believe that there is some reason for all this pain. It's hard to believe when I'm so angry. Whenever I'm alone, when the music and the noise die down, I realize that I'm a very bitter person, and bitter people aren't believers in miracles or angels or providence. But I don't want to be like this forever. I used to look up into the sky at night and say what kids say, "Starlight, star bright, first star I see tonight. . . ." But the wishes that I had never came true. I never felt the kind of security I wished for at home. I never had that knight in shining armor whisk me away on a white horse. I guess that's why I became such a skeptic. I look at my life and I don't like what I see. Will I be able to believe in you? God, why can't I trust you?

In the middle of the cold, starlit night, Troy walked in a field. Exhausted and very disoriented, he didn't know where he was or how he got there. He heard faint laughter and the echoing sound of dogs barking. He heard a voice that seemed to be crying out to him.

"Troy!" The girl's voice echoed through the field as if to pique his curiosity. He ran to the voice. It led down a winding dirt trail, through large trees with branches that shifted and swooned with the cold breeze. Through the steam of his own breath, he saw a faint light ahead. The girl's voice became louder and more defined. He could make out that the light and voice were coming from a spacious home surrounded by a fence of wrought iron and brass. He opened the gate and walked to the door and as he did, the door opened. With some hesitancy he walked in. The music of Nirvana filled the room. He looked over to the wet bar and saw Tad holding a fifth of vodka. Seeing a familiar face, Troy smiled in relief.

"Surprise!" Tad said.

"What kind of party is this?" Troy asked, still confused.

"It's for you, man!"

"Who are these people?"

"They are your friends; it's just kind of dark in here," Tad said as he put his arm around Troy's neck. "The whole gang is back to wish you well in your final high school game!"

"No kidding. I could barely make out that it was you," Troy said.

Troy looked over to his left and there was Chelsea, a girl he dated before she left for college in Missouri. She walked over and kissed him as if they were still dating. "Hey, baby, long time, no see."

"I didn't even know you were in town," he said in astonishment.

"Hey, it's your party. I wouldn't miss it for the world. Here's to great parties . . ." she said as she took a long drag on a joint she held between her thumb and finger. She then passed it to him.

The doorbell rang and through the door he saw the silhouette of Rachel, a girl he had known for years. Two years ago, Rachel and Troy had a fling for a couple of weeks. Their relationship was all or nothing and when the sexual relationship ended, they never spoke to each other again. But tonight she came to him and embraced him. "I've always loved you, Troy. You treated me like dirt after we broke up, but I'm ready to make peace. OK?"

Troy couldn't believe what he was hearing. He took a drag from the joint and soon felt dazed and fatigued. People continued to laugh and talk like he wasn't even there. *If this is a surprise party and I'm the guest of honor, something is definitely weird here,* he thought to himself. He wasn't feeling good at all by this time, and he wanted more than anything to slip out.

Then he felt a cool hand as a girl stroked the back of his head that was damp with cold sweat. It startled him. Troy turned and looked up. A shock surged through his body. *How could this possibly be?* he wondered. Susan Stedham stood before him in the very dress she wore the night they met. "Hi Troy. I've missed you," she said.

Troy's heart raced. He wanted no more of the music, the drugs, the party, and the people. He raced out the door.

"Stop!" demanded a deep subterranean voice. He turned around and saw a cloaked, hulking figure whose face had canine features and pale white skin, more animal than human. As it spoke its teeth bore the resemblance of a wild boar. "This is your destiny, Troy. You will not leave. It is what you have chosen!" the beast shouted. Troy burst through the iron gate and ran through the woods, tripping over vines and broken limbs as he heard the monstrous pounding of the beast's cloven hooves drawing closer and closer to him. The beast no longer called out to him in the pursuit, but growled in anger and rage. Troy felt as if his lungs would collapse when the beast dove and clutched his ankles with its huge callused hands. The beast screamed, "Your choice, young man! Your destiny!"

Troy sat straight up in his bed, his T-shirt dampened with a blanket of sweat. A dream. But the monsters of his life pushed him deeper into a fog of anxiety and fear. He knew that many times, especially at night, he struggled to breathe and battled a cough, trying to convince himself it was a late winter bug. But deep down he wondered, *What is happening to me?*

15

It was Wednesday morning, the day before the game against Western High that would determine the fate of Summit High's playoff hopes. Although Western had secured a position in the playoffs, they wanted this one badly. Western wanted to go to State with momentum and confidence.

Clipper shot free throws before sunrise outside his house, wondering if his aspirations for playing varsity were a big mistake. He loved to play the game, but after those two missed free throws against Woodlawn, Clipper doubted his ability to play in the clutch. If he got fouled and missed both free throws again, he was positive he'd confine himself to a remote village in Bangladesh as a missionary!

His dad walked through the sliding door holding his first cup of coffee, greeting him using his proper name, "Morning, Clifford, you *did* go to bed last night, didn't you? You know there's more to basketball than free throws. There's such a thing as overkill."

"Anything would be an improvement over Saturday night."

"Clipper, you only had two shots at the line. Plus Tupper didn't choose you because you're a free throw shooter. He got you for the rebounding, and you didn't let him down."

"I got a couple of rebounds," he said with self-pity.

"You only played a couple of minutes."

"I saw the game video. I run around like a—" He searched for an appropriate simile, "Let's just put it this way. I looked like a dork."

"Everybody feels that way when they see themselves play on video for the first time," his dad said.

"I just felt like such a loser. Especially compared to how you did."

"What?" Clipper's dad said, surprised.

"You know what I mean. Fifty-four points in one game. You broke every record in the book."

"Not every. Plus that was in North Dakota, not Indiana."

"Yeah, but you were really good. I saw the clippings. You were 84 percent at the line."

Mr. Hayes looked at Clipper and shook his head, "It's all a matter of perspective. If we had the choice between a kid that was an excellent free throw shooter, but went out drinking, never let us know what was going on in his life, wasn't a Christian, or we could have a great rebounder who had trouble with his free throws, but loved the Lord, and respected us as his parents, who do you think we'd pick?"

Clipper continued to stare at the ground. There was comfortable silence between the two. Finally Clipper's dad continued. "Plus, who is to say that two free throws determines the destiny of the rest of your season? You can hit them. I've seen you. Have I ever seen you! At 3:30 in the morning I've seen you do it."

"Not 3:30 A.M.," Clipper said smiling.

"Well close to it."

"I don't know why this whole thing means so much to me. I mean, Justin has it all together. It's like, if he's a failure tomorrow night, he's still on the dean's list, he could date just about any girl at Summit . . . But for me—"

"Clipper! What are you talking about? What does that say about me and your mom? Are we that easily impressed? We think you are the best kid we've ever known, and you just happen to be our kid."

"I guess that's pep talk number thirty-four."

"Nope. It's truth. And you want to hear something else?" Clipper's dad asked.

"I don't think I have a choice," Clipper replied.

"You're right. You don't."

Clipper looked up and smiled.

His dad continued the somewhat embarrassing display of verbal affection, "I love you. And if the time arises that you're at the line tomorrow night, I believe you'll drain 'em." Clipper's dad turned around and headed back inside, calling out as Clipper continued the litany of shots, "Now you'd better get off the line and try some shots in the paint. That's where you'll spend your time tomorrow night if you ask me."

Clipper continued to shoot the ball, imagining with both anticipation and dread what the future might hold. He didn't even know if he would see any playing time. In some ways he hoped that he wouldn't. He whispered a prayer of thanksgiving for his mom and dad. In the past year he had felt closer to them. They'd had their moments of anger in the past, but they weathered those storms. He remembered the times when he couldn't wait to be on his own. He recalled those times when he hated their nagging and their lack of understanding about who he was and who he wasn't and would never be.

He had felt unspoken pressure in the past for him to be someone that he could never be, but this past year he had grown and perhaps they too had grown. He'd always looked upon his dad's glory days with great envy. He wanted to see the all-state trophies in his bedroom like they had been in his father's. But time ran out and it never happened. Still this was his magical moment, small though it may have seemed to others. "Run the race. Finish the course." These few words of Scripture drove him to seek the dream once more.

That morning Kandi saw Justin in the school hall just before the first bell. "Hey, guy, need any help with your locker?"

"You know, you *really* amaze me," Justin said as she walked up.

"How so?"

"You're the only girl I know who's been able to master a locker in the west hall in less than a month. You don't even kick it anymore."

"It's a woman's touch," she said coyly.

"Hmm."

"Plus I had the custodian replace the inner latch."

"Ah ha! That's cheating," Justin said.

Kandi laughed.

"So, are you ready for the game tomorrow?" Kandi asked Justin.

"I don't know. Coach kinda flipped out on us the other day, so he's either motivated us or scared us half to death. I guess we'll find out tomorrow night. Has anybody invited you to the game?"

"No. But it *is* open to the public," Kandi said with a wry smile.

Justin leaned against the lockers casually, "Well, take this as a personal invitation. By the way, I've bought you something." Justin pulled a small box from his front pocket and handed it to her.

Kandi blushed when she opened the box and found a ring. "Justin . . . I'm uh . . . speechless." She was really at a loss for words. *The guy's never asked me out on a date, and he's handing me some kind of ring?* she thought. "A ring?"

Justin immediately could tell that she was taken aback by the gift. "Don't worry. I guess I should have explained it to you before I gave it to you."

"I'm all for explanations."

"See, your dad should really be the one to give you this, but since he's not around, I thought I'd go ahead and do the honors."

Still perplexed Kandi said, "OK, Dad, what's with the ring?"

"It's a commitment ring," Justin said awkwardly. "It's a ring that symbolizes a commitment that you won't have sex with anyone before you're married. I decided last night to give it to you. My parents gave me one a couple of months ago."

"People in Indiana sure do talk about sex a lot. You have Bible studies on it. You wear rings about it—"

"You just came around at the right time. This month it's sex. Next month, water polo."

She smiled, looking at the ring for a few seconds and then placing it on her finger. "So what does this ring make you?"

"Just the guy who had the courage to give it to you. I know you've been through a whole lot since you came here. I really do care about you. I have since I met you."

"Why?"

"'Cause Baby, you and me . . . We got a groovy kind of love."

Kandi laughed at his tongue-in-cheek recitation of one of the hokiest love songs ever recorded. "I just do, Kandi. I care a whole lot about you. I could say that I find you really attractive and fun to be around, which is true." Kandi dropped her head and smiled in embarrassment as he continued. "But the fact is, I think God sort of put me in your path to give you locker tips and rides in the rain."

"That's sweet."

"So will you be at the game tomorrow? That is, of course, if you're not installing software on your computer or bathing the cat."

"I guess the cat can wait. I'll be there."

From the locker room, the Summit High players could hear the rumble and distant cheers coming from the packed house in the gym, the sound of tradition in Indiana. Win or lose, Summit could count on a packed house when Western came calling. The smell of popcorn wafted into every corner of the building.

Clipper jerked Justin down a long row of lockers that were only used during the football season. "Clipper! What the heck are you doing?"

"I've been asking myself that question all day. What am I doing here? Why did I even think that I could be on this team? I'm no good, I tell you. Look at me."

"What?" Justin asked loudly.

"Look at me!"

"I'm looking."

"I'm fritzed out! My heart's pounding. Do you think I'm having a panic attack?" Clipper said, trembling.

Justin tried to remain serious, "A panic attack?"

"Yeah, I saw this thing on '20/20' about panic attacks and—"

"Clipper. You are pumped. You're stoked. This is a big game. I'd call the doctor if you weren't a little nervous. That's the exciting part . . . the fun part."

"This is fun?! This is exciting? Look at me Justin! Do I look like I'm having fun? I'm dyin' here!" Clipper moaned through his gritted teeth, gripping Justin's shoulders and shaking him for emphasis.

Justin peeled Clipper's right hand from his shoulder and spoke calmly. "Clip, just chill. You're beginning to freak *me* out." Justin thought maybe a good slap or ice water on the face might bring his friend to his senses. But he had never done anything like that before and now wasn't the time to try. "OK, Clipper. I want you to cease and desist. You're not starting the game and you'll have time on the bench to sit back and get a feel for the situation. Just take deep breaths and enjoy the game. Coach Tupper might not even need you so—"

"Are you saying that I'm not good enough?"

"Clipper! WHAT IS THE DEAL! First you want to run away to Tahiti and forget that you ever saw a basketball, and now you're upset because I suggest he might not give you any time! Is there anything that'll satisfy you? Look. I am your best friend, right? It doesn't matter what happens out there, you're still going to be the man. Why don't I pray for you?"

"What? Come again?"

"Pray. You do remember prayer, don't you?"

Clipper looked to his left and his right, checking the scene for onlookers, then felt embarrassed. Justin was the new Christian, and he was taking the lead. "Oh yeah," Clipper chuckled nervously, "That's right. We oughta pray."

They sat down on the hard wooden bench bolted to the concrete floor of the locker room. Justin began, "OK, God, Clipper's kind of having some nerve trouble here. What I'd like you to do is help him to chill out and not worry about it. I need that, too. We're both scared about what's going to happen out there. Could you help us just to have a good time and do our best?"

Clipper broke in, "And Lord, keep me off the free throw line."

Justin rolled his eyes as he said, "Amen."

"Hey, Kandi!" Melissa called out, standing up in the bleachers.

"Hey! Thought I'd never find you."

"So you made it."

"This place is crazy," Kandi yelled over the screams and cheers of the fans and the music over the loudspeaker. "Got room?"

"Yeah. Come on over," Melissa said.

"Kandi, do you know Shelli and Myra?"

"I think I've seen you around, but no, I don't think we've met."

Myra, a sophomore at Summit High asked, "Aren't you going out with Troy? He is such a cool guy."

Kandi didn't know what to say at first. She rarely disagreed with strangers. That was simply not her nature. "Yeah, He's definitely . . . a really . . . he's a guy all right," she said not meaning to be funny at first, but they all laughed.

She thought about clarifying the relationship to Myra, but then bit her tongue. Was it really worth going into Troy's true nature? She thought not.

As Melissa, Myra, and Shelli continued the small talk of the team, the happenings at school, and prom, Kandi left the scene mentally, recalling the events of the past couple of weeks, all that she had experienced both good and bad.

She'd grown through the pain, elation, and misery of the past week. She'd had a major confrontation with her mom and a reconciliation. She had fallen for one of the most popular guys in the school in less than two days, then she'd been attacked by him in his own house. She'd been rescued by Justin, who was the kindest guy she'd met, and she'd had an encounter with this Jesus guy, who she had discounted as another mythical icon before that time. But the myth of Jesus walked out of the Bible and lived and breathed and cared for her. That night at Justin's house, as she sang songs about this stranger, she wondered if he could be the dad she had never known? Could he be real? Could he provide an answer to the anger, fear, and frustration that followed her down the path of her life from her earliest memories?

Coach Lunsford's voice roared through the locker room. "Where's Troy! Has anybody seen him?"

Everyone looked at Tad, his best friend on the team. "He was sick today. I called him this morning after second period and he said he'd be here, but not for class."

Tupper walked into the locker room. He stood in the middle of the team, looking as if someone had just shot the president. He cleared his throat and looked at the team. "Troy's not playing tonight."

Lunsford's mouth dropped open. "What do you mean? Where is he?"

"I just got off the phone with Troy's dad," Tupper said. "He can't play?"

"Why not?" Tad asked defensively.

Tupper shouted back, "He's just not going to be able to play. He's sick. He has walking pneumonia. Justin will start tonight in his place. We need to make whatever adjustments—"

Tupper was interrupted by the loud slam of the locker room door.

"I will play. I have to play," Troy said as he walked in the locker room.

"I can't let you do that. You've been restricted by the doctor and your parents," Tupper responded.

"No!" Troy shouted back. He charged at Tupper, but Lunsford and a couple of players tackled him before he got there.

"This is crazy. It's my life. It's my team too. I made this team what it is this year. If I want to end up in the hospital after this, it's my choice!" Troy shouted back while being restrained.

"You're wrong, Troy! Dead wrong. It's tragic. What's happening is tragic, but you are out tonight. You can suit up, but I'm not playing you!"

Silence fell over the team.

"Forget you! Forget all of you!" Troy shouted while struggling to breath. "Guess you told them. I guess you told them I had AIDS! Didn't you?" Troy shouted.

"No, I didn't," Tupper responded. "I said you have pneumonia, which you do. You're the one who said AIDS. Not me."

Troy looked around the room filled with a mixture of humiliation and rage. "Well, if you think for one second that I'm going to sit on the bench and watch Clipper Hayes blow the entire season, you're wrong. What kind of guy do you think I am?"

Lunsford shook his head, "I think you're proving that right now."

"Get him out of here," Tupper said under his breath, trying to restrain his wrath. "Get him out of here right now. We've got a game to play."

Fifteen players and two coaches were in complete shock. Tad felt an ache in the very pit of his stomach as he stared helplessly at his best friend. He was still trying to digest the words that Troy had spoken. AIDS. What would be the aftershock for the rest of their friends, his parents, the girls he had dated?

Myra was the first of the group to notice Troy's absence from the team. "OK, what's up, Kandi? What'd you do with Troy?"

"What did *I* do with Troy?" Kandi asked, genuinely confused.

"He's not out there," Myra explained. "The whole teams doin' that layup thingy, and Troy is not out there."

"How am I supposed to know?" Kandi asked with some exasperation.

"I should have cleared this up earlier, Myra," Melissa interjected. "Kandi and Troy are history. Totally old news."

Myra pouted. "Bummer."

Melissa pulled Kandi closer to her, "I had the strangest conversation today with this girl. I don't think you know her. Her name is Kamden. She's a freshman. She said that Troy was in danger. I haven't even thought about it until now. This is weird."

The news that Troy wouldn't play spread through the crowd and was eventually confirmed by the announcer on the loud speaker. There was an audible collective groan from the audience. Without Troy, the team lacked a competitive point guard. Their slim chance of defeating the already favored Western High Wildcats became even slimmer.

Tupper said to his assistant coach, "I have a feeling deep in my gut that I should have gone with Lester. But you don't count on losing your best guard." He was unaware that Clipper was listening in behind him. Clipper's heart sank. Once again he experienced the second-grade emotions of being picked last in a ball game during recess. He shivered as the crowd reached a fevered pitch during the warm-ups. The noise would rival any college arena.

Justin, noticing Clipper's scowl and lame mood, slapped him on the back.

"What's wrong, Clip. This is what it's all about. Get crankin'."

"I shouldn't be here."

"What?" Justin asked in anger.

"You know what I'm talking about. He should have picked Lester instead of me," Clipper said.

"Would you please stop it!"

"Stop what?"

"Thinking! You can't stop thinking about how you're gonna blow it. I wish you'd just shut up about it," Justin said.

"I heard the coach. He even told Lunsford he shouldn't have picked me."

"So what are you going to do about it? What one thing could change the situation we're in right now? Here's an idea," Justin ranted, totally unaware of the people in the stands, "Why don't you go out there and prove the coach wrong. Believe in yourself for once, Clipper!"

As the game began in the over-crowded, fifty-year-old gym, there was a real feeling that these Summit High students were being led into a pit of lions. Before the season began, the Summit team felt this would be a fun game. They felt that they could compete head to head anywhere with the perennially dominant Western High program, but due to a lack of chemistry and an abundance of injuries, Summit didn't seem to have a chance now. Summit had gotten worse as the year pressed on, and Western kept getting better and better.

Coach Tupper whacked Justin on the rear with the playbook, "OK, Justin. You're starting tonight. You take charge out there. Do you believe in miracles?"

"Yes," Justin smiled reluctantly, "as a matter of fact I do."

"OK. OK, Miracle Boy. Do your thing."

Justin said to himself under his breath, "Do my thing? I don't think I've ever done *my thing* before."

Clipper screamed from the side, "Come on, Justin! All things! Nothin' to lose."

Justin huddled the team near center court before the tip off. "OK. Here we go. Herewego, herewego. Don't let them intimidate you, guys."

They broke into their positions, waiting for the ref to launch the ball, hearts pounding, minds spinning, and nerves tingling.

Clipper on the bench next to Lunsford sent up a silent prayer. "Lord, just let us compete."

During the course of the first quarter, his prayer was answered. Summit High threatened, though they never gained a lead. By the middle of the second quarter, however, Western started to pull away with intimidating fervor, stealing the ball, slamming it home under the basket, and launching threes.

"Clipper," Tupper called out a few seats down on the bench. Clipper was immersed in the game that was quickly turning into a blowout. "CLIPPER!" He yelled at the top of his voice. "Go in for Bryan."

Clipper's heart jumped into his throat as he peeled off his warm-ups and tripped over himself in the process. "All things . . . All things . . ." he kept chanting.

"Uh-oh," Lunsford said to Tupper. "Not a good sign." Both men looked forlorn.

Clipper ran in on defense and immediately snatched a rebound, roaring like a scrawny Hercules.

"Watch it 00," one ref said shaking his finger at Clipper. "Cut the taunting!"

"Sorry, ref. It just came out," Clipper said innocently as he tossed the ball to Justin.

Tad knocked in a wild off-balanced, three-point shot and the home crowd came to life again. Now they began an attack on the twelve-point Western lead. Clipper once again seized the rebound on defense, this time flailing the lethal elbows in order to gain control.

"Hey, boy. What are you trying to do?" one of the Western High Panthers yelled out.

Clipper smiled and tossed the ball to Justin again, then shook his fist in the air to the delight of the home crowd. He couldn't believe it. He was doing it! He knew he could compete and even excel on defense, but his knees weakened on offense. Justin came down with the ball, tossed it to Summit's large center, Antonio, who shot a beautiful hook. The ball softly rolled in and out of the basket.

Clipper and the all-state forward from the Panthers both lunged for the rebound. The Panther, who had been frustrated by this unknown kid, aimed an elbow at Clipper's face in what appeared to be retaliation strike. The referee blew the whistle and rewarded Clipper with a trip to the line. As the referee warned the Panther, and the crowd booed the hard foul, Clipper staggered to the line painfully clutching his nose.

Clipper thought, *What is this? 'National Sock-Me-in-the-Nose Month?!' Can't we all just get along? I'll have the nose of an elephant before the end of the season!*

The referee immediately called an injury time out when he saw a steady stream of blood coming from Clipper's nose.

Lunsford and Tupper both ran out to him. "Hey, kid, welcome to the war, huh?" Tupper said, trying to lift Clipper's spirits. The game had taken a ugly turn, but for Summit it was better than rolling over and playing dead. The bleeding stopped in a matter of seconds, and Clipper went to the line.

Clipper prayed for at least one successful free throw shot, but it was not to be. He missed both and then returned to the bench shortly after to a nice round of applause.

What appeared to be a blowout earlier in the game became a classic battle for respect. Emotions ran high as Summit kept threatening to gain a lead. They had been behind the whole game, but were now within two points in the final seconds of the game. One of Summit's forwards fouled out with only one minute left in the final quarter of action. Clipper was chosen to carry them to the end. He thought to himself as he trotted into the game, *One minute to go; why is Tupper putting me in the game?* The pressure for Clipper was unbelievable.

The Panthers came down the court with the ball. The action slowed for Clipper. With less than forty-five seconds on the game clock, the Western Panthers seemed content to run the shot clock down and sink the next shot to ice the game. The Panther shot bounded off the rim right to Clipper, who tried to rid himself of the ball as quickly as possible before being fouled. He and the Summit faithful breathed a collective sigh of relief when Clipper made a successful pass to Justin. Justin rushed down the court with Clipper right in front of him. He passed the ball to Tad, who pulled up for a three pointer.

The shot arched up and barely hit the rim, landing in Clipper's hands under the basket..

No one in the facility was sitting down as Clipper rocketed up to finish the play with a short basket to tie the game, but before the ball left his hands he was fouled hard by the collective efforts of three Panthers. The Panthers immediately called a time out. With two seconds left, Clipper thought long and hard about the pressure and his terrible reputation as an unsuccessful free throw shooter.

"Great job, men. Ya done good. No matter what happens here. You're a winner. The way you played tonight was . . . a piece off thunder. You never gave up. It was all I asked of you before the game, and you made me proud. Now let's go out there, boys, and send this baby into overtime!"

No one spoke to Clipper, not even Justin. A hushed energy fell over the gym as Clipper set himself for the two most important shots he'd ever taken on a basketball court.

The referee handed him the ball. He bounced it a couple of times. The crowd looked on; everyone was standing.

Clipper's mind went back to those nights in his driveway practicing free throws. His eyes fixed on the basket. "I've had a good game. Come on ball, let's take a ride to the hole," he whispered.

The ball sailed through the air. No one exhaled. Halfway to the basket, it looked great. Clipper's will urged it on. The crowd erupted as the ball rattled in.

Justin, Tad, and Antonio slapped his hands. "You did it, Bro!" Antonio shouted. "OK, baby! It's payback time for the bloody nose," Tad declared.

"You can do all things . . ." Justin whispered in Clipper's ear. *I can do all things through Christ.* That thought filled Clipper's mind and soothed his trembling fingers.

The crowd settled down as the ref tossed him the ball again. The scoreboard read: Western 65, Summit 64. This was his chance to send the game into overtime. Clipper smiled at Justin, and fixed his eyes on the goal once more.

As soon as the ball left his hands, he felt like it would fall through but it hit the front rim. "Nooooo!" he screamed as he lunged for the ball that was well short of the goal.

The rage of the moment tore through his body as he took a giant leap toward the descending ball. The crowd screamed in unanimous panic. His hands reached the ball with one second on the clock. He immediately tossed it skyward. It soared high above with a huge rainbow arch, then came down. Only Newton's theory would determine its fate as it hit the front rim and bounced toward the backboard. The gym floor seemed to vibrate from the incredible screams of the Summit faithful.

In that split second, Clipper couldn't believe what he'd just done. Incredibly, he had gotten the rebound from his own shot and tossed up a prayer. The ball hit the backboard and fell through the basket.

The very foundation of the gym shook as Western stood in shock. The worst free throw shooter Summit had on the squad came to the line hoping to tie the game. The Panthers had already chalked up the victory when Clipper Hayes stole the game right from under their nose.

Justin and the other players rushed toward him as the buzzer sounded, sending him crashing to the floor. Summit

High had pulled off their biggest upset in twenty years. The celebration pile-on knocked the back of Clipper's head on the wooden floor. Clipper didn't care about the growing knot. This was a moment he'd never forget. He wept and whispered his testimony, "All things! I can do all things! Through Christ. Through Christ! Through Christ!"

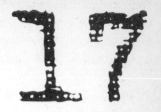

The locker room at Summit High rocked. The team really didn't know how best to celebrate their incredible victory. It wasn't often that high school guys wept tears of joy, but it seemed to be the only emotion they were capable of expressing at the moment. Lunsford tossed Clipper the ball. The same ball he had pushed into the basket with no time left. "This one's on me, Clipper. Here's to our best clutch free throw shooter."

Justin looked around for Troy, wondering if he stayed for the game. He wanted to say that Troy was still a part of the team in his mind, but Troy was nowhere around.

Even though the win was monumental to the team now, the victory would fade into the glory days of the past as each moment swept by. But Justin knew AIDS was not that way. It followed its victim like a shadow. Always hiding behind each corner, a slow dull growl that could turn into a roar within a matter of days, even hours. Troy would find AIDS an unwelcome companion for the rest of his life. He would have to learn about T-cell counts, regular doctor visits and hospital stays, the loss of muscle mass and stamina. *This previously healthy athlete will surely not die an old man,* Justin thought. He would probably leave the world emaciated and gasping for his last brutal breath. Chances were, his parents would outlive him.

Justin pondered what it would be like to be Troy now. He'd often envied Troy, his popularity, the ease at which he played the game, the way the girls were attracted to him. He envied Troy in many ways before the announcement was made in the locker room. And now he had to wonder whether it was cruel fate or the fruit of his lifestyle that had left Troy hopeless and helpless.

It was almost 10:00 when Justin walked out onto the gym floor with duffel bag in hand. The gym rested quietly in stark contrast to the uproarious scene that played out just minutes ago. Only the sounds of brooms and trash collection could be heard now as the custodian and some students began the tedious process of clean up. On the far end of the gym, two students were preparing to push the stands against the wall, which would transform the rustic basketball arena back into an exercise facility.

Kandi sat against the wall waiting for Justin. He walked quickly over to her with a smile on his face, "We did it."

As he came closer, he noticed her smile was forced and her eyes were moist and red. "Kandi? What's the matter?"

"I just heard about Troy. Is it true? He has AIDS?"

"It's true. He told everybody on the team before the game."
Justin sat down next to her. They stared straight ahead, not talking; both were emotionally spent. After a long pause, Kandi's
head dropped and rested on her kneecaps as she sat on the
floor. Justin heard her faintly sob. He looked at her and realized
she was trembling. He felt tears well up in his own eyes.

They were all alone now in the gym, but emotions seemed
to fill every inch of the building. Justin awkwardly wrapped his
arms around her as she remained in an upright fetal position
for a long while. He innately rocked her ever so slightly as
she cried.

Kandi felt warmth and comfort that she hadn't felt in years.
She felt no lust or selfishness in his touch. He stroked her hair
and quieted her spirit.

At first he tried to analyze why she was crying. She never
told him what happened the other day when he picked her up.
He worried momentarily, but then dismissed the inquisitive
thoughts. He cared for her deeply, no matter what had happened that day or any other day. At this moment he was called
to be the personification of the love of God, who accepts his
children no matter what hell the child has endured, no matter
what mistake had been made. He heard God's voice speak
through him. "I know it hurts. Shhh. It's OK. I'm sorry Kandi."

"Why does this hurt so bad?" Kandi said as she unwrapped
her arms from around her knees and wiped her eyes. "I guess
I feel guilty because I hated him so much. He tried to force me
to have sex with him that afternoon. We didn't. So why am I so
scared? Why do I feel so guilty?"

After a while they stood up and walked to Justin's car. Justin fought every desire to hold her hand or embrace her, knowing that she needed a friend now who loved her for who she was. She needed someone at that moment who would look after her and not his own desire for intimacy of any kind.

Kandi continued, "Ever since the Bible study at your house I've been wanting to have the kind of joy that you have, but I don't really think it's possible. My life is so messed up." She struggled to speak as she fought back strong emotion. "I've tried so hard to find some peace. I wish I could just hand over my life to God and let him fix it. But there is so much hate and anger . . . I can't give him that. I can't be good enough. I just can't."

Justin had heard about seeking opportunities to share his faith but this was a spiritual ambush of opportunity! He inventoried his spiritual training, Scriptures that he might know by memory. How he wished he knew more, but he was just a new believer. *Lord, I don't know what to say. I need help here!* he thought to himself.

In the quiet that followed, he felt God saying, *Justin, stay cool. Be honest and tell her what happened to you a few months ago. I'm big enough to carry you on this one if you'll just do what I say and be obedient.*

This wasn't a game or a date. This was life or death for Kandi. She needed to know and Justin knew he needed to tell her. So he told her his story.

He told her about his search for satisfaction through wild parties and social status. He told her about his own feelings of loneliness when his mom left the family and his dad remarried.

"I kept waiting on my fifteenth birthday for my mom to call and just say 'Hi, Happy Birthday.' But it never happened."

Justin recounted how he tried to find some sense of meaning in life through achievement and even relationships, but almost every night he would lie in bed and wonder if this was all there was to it. "I felt there had to be more than this. I wanted to find something, someone who wouldn't run out on me. And I guess that's how I ended up believing in Christ. I had a lot of shame in my life. About what, I don't know. I just felt really alone and shameful. And that's why I had to believe in Christ."

He gave a little laugh. "It's like I didn't have a choice! I was a believer. And when I gave up, surrendered to God's plan, it was like all the guilt and shame of my life just, well, disappeared. I couldn't believe it."

They talked for a few more minutes and then walked out of the gym and into the parking lot. Across the parking lot, they heard a moan.

"I'd better check this out," Justin said.

"Not without me," Kandi said.

They had both had enough excitement to last a few years, but they were compelled to investigate. The sound was coming from under the bleachers of the old Summit High Football field. The moon provided just enough light for them to see someone lying face down in the dirt. They could tell it was Troy.

"Troy?" Justin said softly.

Troy didn't react at first. Then he screamed words that were muffled by the ground. "God! God! God! This is your God, Justin. Your God did this to me."

Justin didn't know what to say.

Troy continued after a long, tense moment, "Why did he let this happen to me. You always said to me . . . everybody said to me . . . that God is love. Why would this loving God do this to me?"

"I don't think he did it, Troy."

Troy got up on his knees and then stood up. He looked at Kandi and Justin with malice. "I guess you're glad you didn't get involved. Right, Kandi? You're thankful, aren't you?"

Kandi looked away. This was not the same confident athlete that had flirted with her just days ago.

"I'm sorry that this happened to you," Kandi whispered.

"What are you doing?" Troy demanded. "You should be celebrating. You hate me. Why don't you say it? You're saying that so you can feel better about yourself. You can say that you have pity on me. Well I don't need your pity, Kandi."

Justin finally spoke. "That's about enough—"

"Nope, Justin, it's not," Troy said with an angry smile on his face. "You still haven't answered my question? If your God loves me, like you say he does, why is he going to kill me."

Kandi spoke loudly, "Stop blaming God! Stop it!" She even surprised herself. She had asked similar questions in the past and now she was impulsively defending this God whom she had doubted most of her life. "God didn't take my Dad's job away. God didn't force him to drink. There's a whole lot of things that happen in this world because we make our own choices. It was your choice to sleep around, Troy. Not God's."

Justin stood there stunned by Kandi's bold statement.

Troy began to weep again as Justin took a step toward him. Before Justin's hand reached his shoulder, Troy ran away.

A few miles away the basketball kept on bouncing at Clipper's house. "OK Clipper. I've put it off just about as long as I can. You've got school in the morning, and I would imagine that you'll need your strength to subdue all the girls who'll want to ask you out after that final play."

"Yeah . . . Right, Dad."

"You did it. Didn't you?"

"I don't think so, Dad. It's like I wasn't even there. I mean I felt it and I freaked when that ball bounced off the goal and all. All I could think of doing was putting the ball back in there. Could you believe what happened?" Clipper continued; the rate of his speaking became swift and energized. "I was so tired and nervous and I couldn't catch my breath and it was like I just—"

"You mounted up with wings of eagles."

"Yeah. That's what it felt like. Wings of eagles. That's a quote from somebody. Right? Abraham Lincoln?"

"Nope. Isaiah. Hey, Clipper, did I ever tell you how proud I am?"

Clipper stopped dribbling and looked directly at his dad as he continued.

"And that really doesn't have anything to do with your game tonight. Nothing whatsoever. I knew you'd be out here, win or lose, and I planned to come out here and tell you that

I'm proud of you. So there. I said it. Now let's get inside before you're grounded."

"Dad, can you give me just five minutes. I'd like to sit out here for a while."

"Five minutes."

Clipper sat down on the swing attached to a huge oak tree in the backyard. He watched the night clouds scuttle across the pale blue moon. He sat motionless, still hearing the frantic and uproarious noise of the crowd that echoed so vividly in the recesses of his mind. In his mind's eye he remembered Justin slapping him on the back. The words his friend said had followed him throughout the year, and he hoped they would follow him throughout his life. "All things, man. All things."

"Lord. I know that I haven't been all you've wanted me to be. And I know I've been blessed. Truly blessed. I guess I'm just beginning to understand what that word *blessed* means. But I know it now. It's getting something from you that we really can't get anywhere else. You didn't have to go out of your way to prove to me about 'all things,' but you did it tonight. Did you ever!" He set the ball down at the base of the goal and headed in for the remainder of the night, thinking to himself, *All things*.

Thanks for visiting Summit High. I'd love to hear from you if you ever want to ask a question, swap stories, need prayer, or even vent about life in general. My E-mail address is

mtullos@bssb.com

See ya!

Matt Tullos